TEMPTED BY HER

CHELSEA M. CAMERON

About Tempted By Her

I wasn't looking forward to finding a new roommate after my best friend, Joy, moved in with her girlfriend, Ezra. We've lived together for years, and I didn't want to start over with a stranger. Then there's a fire at the house Lark's renting and for some reason I open my mouth and offer to let her move in with me.

Lark Conroy, the same woman I had one blisteringly hot night with months ago and have pretended to be normal around ever since. When it comes to love, I'm allergic to romance. I like to hit-it and quit-it and move on with my life.

There's no reason I can't be cordial and normal with Lark while we live together temporarily. We're both mature adults. Well, I'm not that mature, but I can fake it.

Turns out pretending I don't want to kiss Lark every waking moment is harder than I thought, and spending time with her is giving me feelings that I've never had before and don't know what to do with. I'm in a situation and I have absolutely no idea how to stop myself from falling in love with her, or if I even want to.

Chapter One

I DIDN'T INTEND to fuck Lark Conroy—it kind of just happened. I would have blamed alcohol except I'd been completely sober.

After a disastrous meeting with a potential hookup that turned out to be a married couple looking for a third, I'd decided to go on a sexual hiatus for a little while. Having fun with hookups had been my thing for years, and I decided I needed a break.

It had nothing to do with the fact that my two best friends had fallen in love. I was just going on hiatus for a little while.

Focus on myself. Meditate and shit. Whatever.

It wasn't like I wasn't getting off. I was just not getting off with other people to help. My hand and my favorite vibrator were my partners.

Everything was going fine, or at least sort of fine. I was grouchy and having issues sleeping and blowing my cool at work, but I was adjusting. Joy, my best friend, would usually distract me and hug me and bake me something to make me feel better, but she was completely in love with Ezra, the woman she paid to be her wedding date to her sister's wedding. Weird, but who was I to judge?

Left to my own devices, I didn't make the best decisions.

Decisions that led me to end up at a random bar in a random town on a random Friday night. Joy was off with Ezra, and I wouldn't even see her until Monday since they were headed to her sister's wedding.

I'd just needed to get out of Arrowbridge for a bit. Growing up there and then living as an adult in the same town gave me sympathy for goldfish in clear bowls, with everyone watching them and knowing their business.

The bar was dim and a little grungy, which was how bars should be, in my opinion. There was also a grizzled dude wearing flannel sitting at the end of the bar nursing a beer, which a good bar should also have.

The bartender was one of those women who could be thirty or seventy and you couldn't really tell in the low light.

Since I was driving myself, I figured it was best to say sober. One drink would lead to two and that would lead to me potentially being a dumbass.

"Just a Coke with lime, please," I said, and the bartender gave me a disapproving look, but she made the drink and shoved it at me.

"Hi, can I get a rum runner?" a voice said next to me. I thought it sounded familiar, so I turned and found Lark Conroy leaning against the bar next to me.

"Hey," I said, and it took her a second to place me.

"Oh, hey. Sydney, right?"

She and I had met a few times, since she was the sister of Layne's girlfriend, Honor, but I'd never really talked to her. That hadn't stopped me from noticing that she was sexy, though.

"Yeah," I said as the bartender handed Lark her drink with a little more courtesy than she'd shown to mine.

"Do you mind?" Lark asked, pointing to the empty stool next to me. My intention had been to wallow in my misery in this bar alone, but something about the way the light hit her blonde hair and the way her blue eyes looked in the dark made me say, "Not at all."

It was no secret that Lark was gorgeous. Not in that polished and perfect way her sister Honor was. Whereas Honor was designer perfume and stilettos, Lark was messy waves and ripped jeans. Lark was pretty in the way that you imagined what she'd look like in your bed.

I closed my eyes for a second to try and stop that runaway-train of thoughts. It didn't lead anywhere good.

"What brings you here?" she asked, and I decided that a little small talk wouldn't hurt anyone.

"Just out wandering. I got sick of Arrowbridge," I said, sipping my drink and wishing it had alcohol in it.

"You grew up there, right?" she asked, and I was surprised she remembered.

"Yup," I said with a sigh.

"Sounds rough," she said, tilting her body toward me.

"It can be. What are you doing all the way out here?" I asked.

She shrugged. "Had to get away."

"Too many chickens?" I asked and she smiled, making my body zing with awareness of just how pretty she was.

"I keep having nightmares about them murdering me by pecking me to death." I laughed.

Lark's rental was a tiny little house owned by an elderly woman with a chicken fetish, I was convinced. Chickens on the rugs, chickens on the walls, chicken tchotchkes on every available surface. Excessive was an understatement.

"Maybe it's time to move," I said.

She sighed and sipped aggressively at her drink.

"I would, but I'm pretty much broke. I'm sure Layne has told you about my situation," she said, frowning.

"I mean, I know you're working part time and you took a break from school," I said carefully. I didn't want her to feel shitty about her life. I had no room to judge. I'd barely, and I mean *barely*, gotten a marketing degree only to come back home broke to manage my mom's pottery studio, which I could have done even without the degree.

"You can say I dropped out," she said, rolling her eyes.

"If you were just wasting money and it wasn't going toward anything, then dropping out was smart," I said.

She leaned her elbow against the bar and rested her head on her hand.

"You think so?"

There was a twinkle in her eyes that only spelled trouble. With a capital T.

"I do," I said, leaning closer.

"I CAN BARELY STAND to be around them," Lark said. "Like, I'm very happy for my sister but seeing her go from someone who didn't believe in romance or even having feelings to being so in love that she's almost a completely different person is a trip."

"I know what you mean," I said, working on my second drink and wishing it was a shot or several shots instead. "Only Joy didn't completely change personality. She believes in romance even more now, if that was possible."

I loved Joy. I was thrilled for her. But losing her as a roommate was fucking me up more than I wanted to admit. If she asked me how I was doing with it, I told her I was fine. What a shitty friend would I be if I told her the truth? I wasn't going to piss on her happiness, bottom line. So here I was, sober at a bar in a random town.

At least things had gotten less depressing when Lark showed up.

She sighed.

"How's your job?" I asked.

Lark put her hand out and tipped it from side to side. "It's fine, honestly. It's a good job. I'm very grateful to have it. I'm just not so grateful when someone asks me to make a frankendrink that they created in their mind that has twenty ingredients."

I cringed. "Customers can get so entitled. Believe me, I know. I've had people straight up break something and demand a refund a year later. I'm sorry, pottery is fragile and if you let your kids play tackle football in the living room, something might get broken."

Lark snorted.

"You work for your mom, right?" she said.

"Yup," I said with a sigh. "Don't recommend it."

Lark stirred the ice left in her drink. "My mother doesn't believe in working. She only believes in other people working for money and then marrying them. Or marrying someone who didn't work for the money and inherited it. That's the best-case scenario."

I shook my head. "Your mom is something else."

"Believe me, I know. It's taken quite a bit of therapy to get where I am now."

"And where is that?" I asked.

"To a place where I don't think about how much I hate her every single second," Lark said. "I'm a work in progress."

"Aren't we all?"

Lark shook her head. "I don't want to talk about my mother."

"Sorry, didn't mean for the conversation to veer in that direction," I said.

"What direction would you like this to go in?" she asked, and there was no mistaking the flirtation in her voice. I knew via Layne that Lark was queer, and so was I, and the chemistry between us tonight was as obvious as a flashing neon sign.

I leaned back just a tiny bit. "I'm kind of on a break right now," I said, hating the words as they came out of my mouth.

"A break from what?" Lark asked. Her fingers lightly danced on my leg. That was a universal sign that I would have to be completely oblivious to ignore. Lark was trying to take us in a certain direction and under normal circumstances I would be pulling out my car keys and asking if she wanted to go back to her place or mine.

But I was on hiatus. I wasn't doing this. My last couple of hookups had been disasters and I was just…bored. The excitement of being with a stranger had worn off and it almost felt like a thing I did because it was what I'd always done and not because I wanted to.

Lark was…yes, she was hot. She was just my type. Granted, I had many types, but she fit firmly into several categories. Lark also wasn't a stranger, and hooking up with her could get complicated. She had an intensely protective older sister, and I didn't want to get on Honor's bad side, even if Lark was an adult who could make her own decisions. Familial relationships were complex like that.

"This," I said, gesturing between us. "I'm kind of taking a hiatus from hookups."

Lark raised one eyebrow but didn't remove her hand from my leg. My skin tingled under my jeans where she touched, and it was seriously distracting.

"Oh, a hookup hiatus, huh?" she said, and this time she was almost completely in my lap. I knew, without a doubt, if I told her to stop touching me that she would.

I couldn't seem to find the words to tell her to stop because I didn't want her to stop.

"It's supposed to be," I said, licking my lips." But I'm feeling like I might need a hiatus from my hiatus."

Lark thought about that for a second. "So what does that mean for me?"

I took a breath and let it out. "It means that I'm sober and I'd like to take you home with me."

Lark smiled slowly.

"We're definitely going in the right direction now."

THE DRIVE back to my apartment took longer than I thought it would, because I didn't really know how to get there from the bar, and my GPS didn't seem to either. At last, I recognized where I was and drove as fast as I dared to get to Arrowbridge.

I parked my car in the designated space and looked over at Lark.

"If you don't want to come up, I can take you home," I said, giving her a chance to escape if she wanted it.

She shook her head. "Let's go."

Just as I was unlocking the door, Joy sent me a text message from the rehearsal dinner at her sister's wedding. She and Ezra both smiled as Joy smushed their faces together.

I sighed and opened the door. Clementine, my fluffy orange cat was right there waiting to see me.

"Hello, yes I know," I said, leaning down to give him attention.

"Aw, he's so sweet," Lark said, leaning down. She put her hand out tentatively to Clementine, who studied this new person with a critical gaze before going over to sniff her fingers and then shove his head against her hand.

"Ohhh," she said, letting out the cutest little squeal. "I think he likes me."

The sound did something to my body that had nothing to do with lust. I ignored it.

"He has good taste," I said, standing up. "Do you want anything else to drink?"

"Water would be good, I think," she said. "I'm trying to be responsible."

"Responsible?" I asked as I opened the fridge. "What is that like?"

"Hey, you're the one on a hookup hiatus," she said as I poured both of us a glass of water from the filtered pitcher. "Sounds pretty responsible to me."

"It's not going well at the moment," I said, handing her the glass. She took it from my fingers and our eyes met. I had to clench the glass so I didn't just drop it.

Lark Conroy was very, very much my type.

"Thanks," she said, taking the water from me and gulping it down. "Do you want to know something?"

I moved away from her so I didn't kiss her. "I'd love to know something." I reached for my own water, hoping it could cool the fire that kept burning brighter the longer we spent together.

"Tonight was my first time at a bar. Legally anyway," she said. That stopped me for a second.

"Wait, how old are you?" I guess I'd just assumed we were the same age.

"Twenty-one," she said. "As of two weeks ago."

I cleared my throat. "Well, happy belated birthday."

"Thanks," she said. "Is it rude to ask how old you are? I don't want to assume."

"I'm twenty-six," I said. She seemed visibly relieved. "Are you not into MILFs?"

Lark almost choked on her water. "No, I am. I mean…" she trailed off, her face red.

"It's okay, Lark," I said, enjoying saying her name.

She set her water glass down on the counter and stepped toward me.

"How's your hookup-hiatus hiatus going now?" she asked, tucking one of my curls behind my ear.

"Oh, I think it's progressing nicely," I said, stepping closer and putting my hand on her waist to pull her body flush with mine. Lark was just a few inches taller than me and I liked that. She looked down at me and smiled.

"So we're going in the right direction?"

"Yes," I said before I tilted my face to meet her mouth. The kiss exploded in my brain like fireworks. I really hadn't been on my hiatus that long, but it felt like I hadn't had a physical touch in a thousand years. I needed this kiss like oxygen and water and sustenance all rolled into one.

Lark trembled just a little bit and I lifted my hand to her hair as I pushed her a little, running my tongue along the seam of her lips, asking for entry.

She opened to me immediately, and that was all it took before I was backing her toward my room. Sure, we almost tripped over furniture and the cat, but we made it there in the end.

"I hate clothes," I said between kisses as I pulled at hers. Normally I was excellent at peeling off any kind of outfit in a few seconds or less, but my fingers were not cooperating with me tonight.

"Me too," Lark said. She'd been just as desperate to get mine off and had made just about as much progress.

A loud meow interrupted us, and I looked down to find Clementine rubbing himself against my legs and wailing.

"Pause button," I said to Lark and stumbled to the kitchen and tried to remember how to put cat food in a bowl. There wasn't much blood in my brain right now since it had migrated to more important areas. At last, the cat was fed and I went back to the bedroom to find Lark looking at my bookshelves.

She faced me, her cheeks flushed and pretty. "Still hate clothes?"

"More than ever," I said.

Lark laughed and pulled her shirt over her head. Her bra was simple but classic—soft beige cotton. "Your turn."

I didn't really care who got naked first, as long as she got naked as soon as possible, so I yanked my shirt over my head and thanked past Sydney for always buying underwear that I wouldn't mind someone else seeing. The dark blue lace made me feel sexy when I wore it.

"Should I leave these on?" Lark said, pointing to her jeans.

"Absolutely not," I said, and she laughed as she pulled them off. I watched her reveal a pair of black underwear.

"I didn't think anyone was going to see these," she said, gesturing at the mismatch.

"I don't care about those. I care what's under them," I said as I removed my own jeans. The blue lace boyshorts didn't cover much. They were basically decorative instead of functional, which was exactly how I liked them.

"Fuck, you're hot," Lark said in a way that was almost wistful. She was so cute.

"Wanna touch?" I asked.

"Yes, please," she said, and we came together again, almost tripping over the clothes we'd discarded in an effort to get to my bed.

Lark ended up on her back and I straddled her. When it came to sex, I did love topping, but I was pretty flexible if we were both on board.

I couldn't seem to go slow with Lark. One hand yanked on her underwear while the other I used to prop myself up as I devoured her mouth and sucked on her lips and caressed her tongue with mine.

Fuck, it had been a long time since I had been on fire like this. I'd missed it. Lark was exactly what I'd needed tonight.

Somehow, I got my head together to get her completely naked and I took a moment to take her in.

"You are something else," I said. I couldn't wait to get my hands and tongue all over her. "Is there anything you don't like?"

Sex was always better when everyone was on the same page.

"Um, it's been a little while for me," she said, suddenly blushing and covering her chest. "How about I let you know?"

"Works for me," I said. "My feet are really ticklish, so if you're into toes or feet, I don't know if that will work for me." I always mentioned that due to an incident with a previous partner that ended in a broken nose, lots of blood, and an emergency room visit. Never again.

"Oh, uh, I'm not," she said.

I shrugged. "Either way."

Lark seemed to be studying my face. "What is it?"

"Nothing."

"Do you want to stop?"

She still had her hands covering her boobs.

Lark shook her head. "Hell no."

I grinned down at her. "Want me to get naked?"

She nodded eagerly. "Yes, fuck, yes."

It only took a few seconds for me to unhook my bra and shimmy out of my underwear.

"Oh my god, your body is amazing," Lark said.

"Yours is fucking perfection," I said. Lark's boobs were heavy, and I couldn't wait to cup them in my hands and feel their weight. Her stomach was soft and rounded, her hips curved and perfect for holding onto. I wondered if her shyness was due to her personality (which wasn't shy from what I could tell so far), or inexperience. I also wondered if she'd be up for letting me fuck her with my strap-on. I'd just gotten a new dildo I wanted to try out. Joy didn't know it, but I'd found Ezra's sex toy review blog and had bought a bunch of new things to add to my collection based on her recommendations. Plus, the dildo was purple and sparkly.

"Can I touch you?" I asked, leaning down and kissing her softly.

"Yes," she said into my mouth.

Whereas before we'd gotten naked, I'd been sure this was going to be quick and dirty, now the pace had changed. Lark either wasn't ready for quick and dirty, or she didn't want it. That was okay. I could go slow. I could go whatever pace she wanted, as long as we kept going in the same direction.

I brushed my fingers across one of her nipples as I moved from her mouth to her neck. Her breath caught and she let out a little moan that I'd been waiting to hear. There was nothing better, except for maybe hearing her scream my name as she came.

Her nipple hardened and she arched her back a little bit, seeking my touch. Mmm, I liked that too.

I scraped my teeth along her neck where her heartbeat pulsed. Her hands flew to dive into my hair, and I felt her pushing, probably unaware she was doing it.

"Do you want my mouth here?" I asked, circling her nipple with my finger.

"Yes," she gasped, her fingers clenching. If she wanted to rip my hair out, she could go right ahead. I'd just wear a bunch of hats while it grew back. There was a lot I was willing to deal with when it came to getting off.

I watched her face as I moved my way down her body and made eye contact as I stuck my tongue out and flicked it against her nipple. Her entire body jumped, just from that one little touch. I put my hand on her hip.

"Easy," I said.

"Sorry," she said.

"You don't have to apologize, love," I said. Generally, I didn't use terms of endearment because what use was there giving them out when you were never going to see the person again? But it was completely natural to call Lark "love."

"Sorry," Lark said again, and I laughed and then sucked her nipple into my mouth. Her reaction was instantaneous and intense. One hand stayed on my head and the other slapped at the bed and fisted the covers.

She didn't start pleading until I used my teeth to gently bite her. Lark was so responsive, and it was such a turn on. I was so close already, if I shifted my body I could probably come on her leg with just a little bit of careful movement.

Later. I'd get to come later.

Lark's hips started pumping against me, as if she couldn't help herself.

"Do you need me to make you come?" I asked, looking up at her. Lark's eyes were closed and she was straining, reaching.

"Yes," she gasped.

Seeing her so undone was an aphrodisiac, so I moved, leaving a trail of kisses down her body. I nuzzled her belly, but there would be time to kiss her there later. Now she needed me to help her.

"Do you need my fingers or my mouth or both?" I asked.

"Fuck, both," she said, pushing her hips up.

"That's great, because I've been dying to taste you," I said, pushing her thighs apart and getting into a comfortable position. I had a pillow wedge that could be used for better access, but I didn't want to leave her to go get it from under my bed.

I shifted her a little bit and then I stroked her with my hand.

"Oh god," she said. "Please, Sydney. Please."

I loved hearing her beg me. It was so fucking sweet.

I fluttered my fingers across her and then I couldn't wait anymore and licked her up and down. Maybe I should have been gentler, but Lark didn't seem to mind as she pushed my head closer, making me smile.

Her taste was perfect as I flicked my tongue around her clit, looking for the exact right spot that would make her go off like a firework.

Her sounds and her movements told me when I had found the promised land. I made note of the location before targeting a different area to push her higher. She was drenched and dripping all over my comforter. Good thing I had a backup in my closet.

"I'm going to use one finger," I said. "Tell me if it's too much, or if you need more."

Her only answer was a moan, but that worked well enough for me.

My finger slid easily into her, and I immediately searched for her g-spot. I knew I'd found it by touch, and by her entire body seizing up when I stroked it.

"Close," she gasped.

I could feel her body drawing tighter and tighter like a bow ready for release. Not that I'd ever done archery, but I'd seen enough movies.

Desperate to see her come, I added a second finger and worked my tongue furiously as she trembled from head to toe and then her entire body seized and she cried out in the sweetest, sexiest way that was so real and so pure that I wished I could bottle it.

Lark came and came, and I was feeling pretty good about myself after her body finally stilled and her eyes opened.

"You're gorgeous," I said, which was the first thing that came to my mind.

Lark breathed heavily and a soft smile spread on her face. Fuck, she really was beautiful. So much that I wanted to look away, but I didn't.

"Kiss me," she said in a soft voice, and I did. Her body was warm and sweaty and languid, and I rolled us so we were on our sides.

"What do you need?" she asked after we kissed for a few moments.

"After watching you? Not much," I said, taking her hand, and running it down my stomach before letting go and giving her the chance to do what she wanted with me.

"I want to taste you, too," she said.

I rolled onto my back and spread my thighs.

"Go ahead, love," I said.

Lark sat up, her hair complete chaos. Even more so than mine. She had a huge smile on her face, as if I'd just gifted her with a special gift.

"Actually," she said, licking her lips. "Can you sit on my face?"

This was shaping up to be the greatest night of my life, and I'd had a lot of great nights.

"Fuck yeah I can," I said, sitting up and helping her arrange herself on my pillows so she was comfortable.

"Ready?" I asked her. She nodded and I straddled the top of her chest and grabbed onto my bed frame. The bed frame I'd specifically chosen for activities like this. The guy at the discount store had been a little taken aback when I asked how sturdy it was.

"In case of an earthquake or hurricane," I'd said, but I knew he didn't believe me.

The first touch of Lark's tongue made me want to just grind mercilessly against her face, but I held myself back as best I could, letting her take the lead.

While the first lick seemed like a test, the second, third, and everything after that felt like a mission. Lark's mission was to destroy me in the process of getting me off, and I was going to let her. Lark's fingers dug into my hips, urging me to move. To use her mouth.

"Goddamn, you're perfect," I said as I thrust against her eager tongue. She made a sound of satisfaction and that was all it took for me to completely surrender to my body and the sweet inevitable clutch of a powerful climax that started hard and just got harder as I seized against her mouth. I hadn't come like this, with stars bursting behind my eyes, in ages. Not all orgasms were created equal and this one was an inferno, whereas others were like little sparks.

Once my body quieted down, I looked down to make sure I hadn't suffocated Lark as I'd been coming.

I leaned back and rested on her chest again.

She smiled up at me, her face wet.

"Thank you," she said, licking my taste from her lips.

"You're welcome," I said, at a loss for any other words.

Chapter Two

THREE MONTHS LATER...

"I can give you some money," Joy said as we ate lunch together. Even though we weren't living together anymore, we still ate lunch together every Monday, as we had pretty much since we'd moved in together six years ago.

"No way. I don't need money," I said. I mean, that wasn't entirely true. Carrying both halves of the rent while I searched for a roommate was a challenge, and it was starting to break me. There were a few days where I had absolutely nothing in my bank account until payday, and I'd been in the hole a few times. I hadn't told Joy about that, because I didn't want her to offer to give me money. Like she was doing right now.

"I'm fine. I'm going to find someone," I said.

"You will," Joy said, nodding with confidence. "You might just have to lower some of your expectations."

"Are you saying my expectations are too high?" I asked. "I'm not that picky."

Joy gave me a look. "I love you, but you're not going to find someone if you're unwilling to compromise."

"I'm not unwilling to compromise." I just didn't want to

live with someone who I couldn't get along with. I knew that I'd won the roommate lottery with Joy, and I was unlikely to find someone like her again, but I did have some standards and people just didn't seem to meet them. There also weren't lines of people in the small town of Arrowbridge needing room-mates, so the pool of applicants was already shallow.

I stabbed at a crouton in my salad with frustration.

"Please let me know if you need help," Joy said. "I've got a little bit of emergency money stashed."

Joy really was the best, and not just as a roommate. She was a good person, through and through. Sometimes that led her to giving people the benefit of the doubt that they didn't deserve. That's where I came in.

"It'll be fine," I said, which was something I'd been saying a lot lately. I was sick of the word fine, and I was tired of hearing it from my own mouth.

Joy's phone went off and she frowned as she looked at it. "It's Layne. Huh."

She answered and her eyes went wide. "Holy shit, is there anything we can do?" She listened and nodded. "Yeah, of course, that's awful. Tell her that whatever she needs, clothes, or anything, we can help. Okay... Okay... Bye."

Joy hung up and set her phone down. "There was a fire at the chicken house a few hours ago. They don't know what happened, probably some bad wiring. Lark was at work, thank god, so she's fine, but just about everything she owned is gone. I can't imagine what she's going through right now."

Lark. I'd tried not to think about her, but I failed just about every time. She'd stayed that night with me, and we'd spent the entire night fucking until the morning when I'd messaged Joy in a panic. She'd called while Lark was still in my bed, but I'd changed my mind about telling her. I wasn't one to keep secrets from Joy, but I'd sealed my lips on my night with Lark, and had done my best to put her out of my mind. To her credit, she'd kissed me and told me she'd had a good time and that had been that. Seemed like we had both gotten what we'd wanted out of that night. I didn't even know how she'd gotten her car back, and I hadn't had her number to ask her.

"Shit, that's horrible. Does she need anything?" I asked.

"Layne's going to let me know. She and Honor are with her and I'm sure Mark and Sadie will pitch in. They've got extra rooms, too."

That was true. Mark and Sadie were RICH rich, and Sadie ran a clothing boutique just down the street in downtown Arrowbridge, so Lark was probably covered in funds and clothing for now. I didn't really have anything I could offer to help that she couldn't get from someone closer to her. A one-night stand did not a relationship make, and I preferred it that way.

"Poor Lark. I can't imagine losing all of my stuff," Joy said, shivering. "Now I have to make sure Ezra has renter's insurance."

"I should probably get that," I said.

"Syd!" Joy said. "You told me you had it!"

"I meant to get it. Does that not count?" I said.

Joy admonished me with a finger. "Syd. Do it right now." For someone who was the youngest in her family, she really had first-born daughter energy.

"Fine, fine," I said, abandoning my salad to look for renter's insurance on my phone.

Joy didn't let up until I showed her the email with my new policy attached.

"Thank you," she said.

"You don't have to take care of me now. Save some of that shit for Ezra," I said.

At the mention of her girlfriend, Joy sighed happily. "She doesn't need much taking care of when it comes to most things."

No, Ezra had her life together, but when it came to love, she needed a lot of help. Joy called Ezra her lone wolf that didn't know how to behave in her new pack and I had to agree. At least my personal relationships were all super healthy. Well, healthy-ish.

I couldn't stop thinking about Lark as I reorganized one of the displays in the shop that afternoon. My mother was ensconced in the back creating all the pottery that she then painted, fired, and finished before it was given to my custody to arrange and sell to the best of my abilities.

Bluebird Pottery specialized in all manner of plates, bowls, platters, lamps, jugs, cups, mugs, and ornaments painted with birds, yes, but other Maine scenes like lighthouses, lobsters, and blueberries. I kept trying to convince her to do a potato line, but she shot down that idea as "not on brand." Funny, because I had literally taught her what "on brand" meant in the first place.

Eileen, my mother, was good at a whole lot of things, but selling the stuff she made wasn't one of those skills. When I was growing up, she'd basically been a "pay what you can" store in the garage of our home, and she'd even accepted trades. Dad had never been around, and Mom had never been shy about telling me that they'd been a drunken hookup and that she didn't need or miss him. She'd never really asked me if I'd missed having a dad, and I'd never talked to her about it either.

The door opened and I turned with my best unthreatening, but welcoming, smile.

"Hello," I said, testing the new customers. They both gave me bland smiles and continued their conversation. I let them do their thing. They smelled like browsers, who were usually just killing time, and it might not be worth it to work my magic on them.

After a few minutes, I checked in and said that they could

let me know if they needed any help. I got more polite smiles. Got it. Message received. I went back to what I was doing and moved on to the next area I had on my long list to handle today. Every day I made a list and every day something happened so I couldn't stick to that list.

There was a loud crash that didn't make me jump because I was used to a lot of loud crashes.

"Excuse me," I said to the browsers, who were now just standing in the middle of the store and talking about their dinner plans. "There's coffee or tea if you'd like," I added, gesturing to the little drink station I'd set up to reward anyone who came in when the weather got colder.

"Any injuries?" I asked as I pushed the door between the studio and the shop almost all the way closed so I could watch the browsers and run out if anyone else walked in.

Mom looked up at me. She'd been staring down at the mug that was now in pieces on the floor.

"Just a mug today? We're doing good," I said. Mom sighed.

"They just jump out of my hands sometimes," she said, blinking at me from behind her glasses. She always got into a sort of meditative state when she worked, and sometimes she was a little dreamy for a while. I got the broom and swept up as I did every day. Just part of the job.

"Have you thought any more about what I said about hiring someone part time?" I asked. Right now, it was just the two of us and Mom wouldn't let me work more than forty hours a week, so she was alone on the weekends a lot and I always came back to chaos on Mondays. The shop was doing well enough to hire someone to help on my days off, and to help with shipping. We could only ship mugs and ornaments because there just wasn't time to do anything else, and we were missing out on so much potential business.

"Mmm," Mom said, the sound non-committal. I heard the

shop door open, so I couldn't continue this conversation with Mom.

"We've got to hire someone. We're drowning," I said, for what felt like the thousandth time.

"Uh huh," Mom said, going back to her clay. As usual.

WHILE I TRIED to keep everything together at work, I couldn't stop thinking about Lark, so I sent Layne a message to give to her that if she needed something to let me know.

She's pretty shaken up right now. Took her back home and put her to bed on the pullout and I'm making her some dinner she replied.

I should have known Layne was already cooking for her. Layne pretty much thought every problem in life could be served by a decent dinner and some baked goods.

Well, I do have an extra bedroom, if she decides she wants to go somewhere else. Joy left her bed and most of her stuff here, so all it needs is some new sheets I sent.

I'd thought about my extra room immediately when Joy had told me about the fire. It seemed like such an obvious solution. Lark had only been renting the chicken house, so it wasn't like she could just rebuild it. She needed a new place to live, fast.

And I needed a roommate. I absolutely didn't believe in any kind of fate, but this seemed like a problem with a solution already available.

If Lark considered staying, even for a little while, I hoped she didn't think that things would be awkward between us. I wasn't used to seeing my hookups ever again, but it could work. We were both adults.

I'll let her know. That's really generous, thanks Syd she responded.

It didn't seem that generous to me. I'd be a complete asshole not to offer. I mean, I could be an asshole about a lot of things, but not about this.

No problem I sent.

Mom and I closed up the shop for the day and I swung by Mainely Books to see Joy again and get any update on Lark.

"Hey," she said. "I know it's not the most important thing, but I grabbed some books for Lark." Of course she had. Joy was such a sweetheart.

"What do you think?" She showed me a small stack that she'd set aside along with some t-shirts and sweatshirts with the bookstore logo and various silly reading quotes and jokes on them. "Kendra said to take whatever I needed. Layne told me she had insurance, but that might take a while to process and she needs a lot of things immediately, so she's going to put up a fundraiser online." I could just picture Layne organizing that while Honor dealt with the insurance company.

"What about a toothbrush and soap and that kind of thing? Do you think Layne has that covered?" I asked.

"Oh, that's a good idea. I feel like she was just dealing with more immediate stuff. Do you want to go to the grocery store and grab some things and we can drop them off with the books?" Joy asked. I should have said no. I shouldn't get involved. There were plenty of other people who were probably handling it.

"I'll drive," I said.

BECAUSE THE LOCAL grocery store was small and didn't have a lot of variety, I drove out to the fancier store outside of Arrowbridge that had a better cosmetics department. I had no idea if Lark needed sheet masks, but I tossed some in the cart and kept moving.

I also didn't know if she had sensitive skin, so I made sure to get anything that seemed super gentle.

"Floss, mouthwash, toothpaste, toothbrush," Joy said, listing off what we'd already gotten on the list she'd made while we drove over.

In addition to the basics, I grabbed a pair of slippers and a robe and even started shoving chips and candy bars and snacks into the cart. It didn't matter if she hadn't asked for that stuff, she was getting just about everything in the store. Joy didn't comment about me going overboard, mostly because she was used to me going overboard after so many years as friends. I just didn't want to miss anything. Sometimes you got into a situation where someone said, "I wish we had a Phillips head screwdriver" and I'd be there with a set of screwdrivers that had been hanging out in my trunk for just that situation.

"Okay, that's everything," Joy said, steering me toward the cash registers. I pulled every trashy magazine off the rack and added them too. Lark was probably going to need a distraction, even though Joy was already bringing her books. Joy had stopped me before I'd headed to the toy section to grab some board games, but I had gotten a deck of cards at least.

I shoved Joy out of the way and used my card before she could stop me.

"I'm sending you money right now," she said, pulling out her phone. A few seconds later, I had a notification that Joy had sent me half of the total. I grumbled as we took the bags out to the car and put them in the back.

Joy ignored me as we drove to Layne's. It was a short trip, and there were lots of cars in the driveway when we got there.

Joy and I headed to the guest house and found a ton of people already there, including Liam, Layne's brother, and his girlfriend, Gwen. Liam was also Lark's boss at the coffee shop, so that was sweet that he'd come to offer support.

"We come bearing gifts," Joy said, smiling as we walked in, weighed down by all the crap we'd bought.

My eyes went immediately to Lark, who was sitting on the couch and staring off into space. I'd never seen her eyes so blank before. I had no idea what she was going through, but if it was me, I'd probably want a few less people staring at me.

"Thank you so much," Layne said, coming over and taking some of the bags from Joy and looking through them.

"Hey, how are you doing?" Joy said with a soft voice, sitting down next to Lark.

"I'm fucking great," Lark said, her voice dripping with sarcasm. She closed her eyes and rubbed her forehead with her hand. "I'm sorry. I'm just… Fuck."

"It's okay," Joy said. "It's a lot to process."

She got up and I knew it was my turn to say something, but I couldn't find the right words.

"There's magazines in there," I said, and then realized that was definitely not the right thing to say. "And gum. And chocolate, if you need it."

Lark actually looked up and met my eyes.

"Thank you," she said softly.

"You're welcome," I said.

"I'm going to make some tea," Honor said. She'd been typing on her phone, probably dealing with the administrative side of things.

"Do they know yet what happened?" Joy asked Layne.

She shook her head. "No, they still need to do an investigation, but everything is pointing to old or bad wiring. Lorna had some random electrician fiddle around years ago and who knows what the hell he did."

Lorna was the owner of the chicken house and lived next

door. She was about a thousand years old, but still completely with it.

"Her house was okay, thank goodness," Layne said. "It just so happened that one of the volunteer firefighters had dropped by to get some eggs from Lorna."

"Wow, talk about right place right time," Joy said. Layne nodded.

"I know."

They chatted about this and that, but I was too busy looking at Lark. She still seemed completely zoned out. All I wanted to do was tell everyone to leave and put her to bed with some sleep aids so she could just knock herself out for a day or so.

Liam and Gwen left, saying that Lark shouldn't worry about her job, and then Honor came in to ask me and Joy if we were staying.

"I think we should ask Lark if she wants us to," I blurted out.

She glanced up at the sound of her name.

"Whatever," she said, closing her eyes.

I pulled Joy aside. "I think we should let her rest. She's clearly exhausted."

Just as I said that, Lark yawned.

Joy nodded and told Honor that we should get going, but to absolutely let us know if they needed anything else.

"Kendra is ready to start a collection at the bookstore," Joy said. "Just say the word."

"Oh, for sure," Layne said, giving both of us hugs. "We'll let you know about crowdfunding and all that."

"And if she needs any plates or mugs or anything, we've got her covered. Ask her if she wants blueberries, lobsters, moose, or lighthouses," I said.

"You're so sweet, I will," Layne said with a sigh. "It's been a long day, but we're handling it. The twins have already made her a bunch of necklaces and bracelets."

I hadn't noticed the bracelets and the beaded necklaces Lark had around her neck.

"Too cute," Joy said.

"I know," Layne said.

Joy and I left and got back in my car.

"You should just ask Lark to move in with you," Joy said. "I mean, she's going to need a new place, and you have an extra room."

"Yeah, I thought of that," I said.

"I mean, you already know her a little bit and you like her, right?"

Liking her wasn't the problem.

"Yeah," I said, pretending to be nonchalant about this conversation.

"There you go. A solution to your roommate dilemma."

Chapter Three

WHEN I GOT BACK HOME, I texted Layne to let her know that if/when Lark needed a place to go, I was open to her being my roommate. She sent back that she was going to ask me if that would be a possibility, but she hadn't wanted to throw it at me in front of everyone.

Well I'm not having much luck finding someone, and I'm happy to give her a tour and talk about money and so forth I sent. Not that she'd need a tour, since she'd already been here three months ago, but Layne didn't know about that.

Layne told me that she'd pitch the idea to Lark when she woke up and also gave me Lark's number so we could talk directly.

I was glad she was getting some sleep, and now all I had to do was wait and see if I was getting a new roommate or not.

∿

THE NEXT DAY I heard from Lark.

Thanks for offering to let me live with you, but I don't think it's a good idea she sent without preamble.

The shop was empty, so I didn't feel weird about messaging her back right away.

Why is it not a good idea? The rent is pretty cheap and I'm guessing you don't have a lot of options I responded and hoped that didn't sound too bitchy, but it was true. Arrowbridge had plenty of homes for sale, but not a lot of apartments for rent.

You know why it's not a good idea, Sydney she sent.

If you're thinking we can't be roommates because of something that happened months ago, then fine. It's not a big deal to me, just so you know I responded.

She didn't say anything for a long time, so I went back to pulling items from the shelves to fill online mug orders.

It's not a big deal to me, I just wasn't sure how you felt about it. If you think it will be fine, then okay. Like you said, I don't have a lot of options she finally sent.

I'm absolutely fine about it. You're totally welcome to move in I replied and sent her the cost for half the rent and utilities.

I can swing that. It's actually cheaper than the chicken house was she sent.

We negotiated a little more back and forth and I said she could come by this week and make sure she wanted to move in.

The two of us agreed on Wednesday night and I said I'd reach out to the landlord and put Lark in touch.

I went to Joy's former room and looked in, imagining Lark sitting on the bed and filling the bookshelves and putting her clothes in the closet. We'd be sharing a bathroom, which was quite a way to get to know someone. I tested the mattress and it was a little old. Joy had been talking about getting a new one for months.

Chewing my lip, I pulled up a few mattress sites and just went ahead and bought one without thinking about it, putting the charge on my credit card. Now I just had to dispose of the old one, so I sent an email to the local junk guy that everyone used asking if he could come this week and deal with a mattress.

Lark had lost everything. She deserved a new mattress.

FOR THE NEXT TWO DAYS, I couldn't stop thinking about Lark, no matter how hard I tried. I wondered what she was doing, how she was doing with the loss. Normally I wasn't one to ruminate on people I'd slept with, and I didn't like this feeling, this stress.

Business was slow at the shop, but our online orders were doing well, even after the November and December holidays, so that kept me busy. Packing the boxes was kind of meditative, but I didn't want meditative right now. All my thoughts seemed to lead back to Lark.

On Wednesday evening before she arrived, I went through the apartment again. The new mattress wasn't here yet, but the old one was gone. I lit a candle to make the place smell nice and used the lint roller on the couch to get rid of the extra cat hair. Hopefully Lark wouldn't mind cat hair everywhere.

"You ready to have a new roommate?" I asked Clementine. He'd been fine with Lark the last time she'd been here and had even climbed into bed with us.

Memories from that night and the following morning wouldn't stop bubbling up.

It was easy. I'd just have to get over it. Living with Lark day-to-day would desensitize me to her presence in no time.

I jumped at a knock on the door and Clementine followed me as I opened it.

"Hey," I said as she stood on the landing in her winter coat and hat.

"Hey," she said, looking a little nervous.

"Come in," I said, holding Clementine back with one foot as I opened the door to let her in.

"Thanks," she said, stamping off her boots and then coming inside.

"Hello again," she said to Clementine, letting him rub up against her hand after she took off her gloves. He seemed to recognize her and started purring immediately.

She stood up and I didn't know what to say for a second.

"Uh, so this is the room," I said, walking toward Joy's old room and opening the door. "There's a new mattress coming. The old one needed to go." That wasn't precisely true, but I didn't want to make a bigger deal out of the new mattress than it was.

I stepped aside so she could walk around. The space wasn't huge, but it was enough, and there was a nice window onto the street.

"You probably remember the rest of the place," I said, and she met my eyes.

"I do," she said, running a finger along the bookshelf.

"How are you doing?" I asked, telling myself it was only polite to ask.

Lark sighed. "On one hand, I don't have to live in a house full of chickens everywhere anymore. On the other, my favorite pair of jeans that exactly conformed to my butt is gone," she said. It took all of my willpower not to look at her butt when she mentioned it. Having seen it myself, I could vouch for it being an excellent one.

This was not the time to be thinking about Lark's butt.

I cleared my throat. "That fucking sucks."

Lark nodded. "It does."

We walked back out to the living room and I sat on the

couch. She took the other end, and Clem jumped up between us to get as much attention as possible.

"Do you want some water or tea or anything?" I asked.

"I've had enough of both. Do you have any shots?" she asked, rubbing her forehead.

"Maybe?" I said, getting up. I didn't know what kind of booze I had off the top of my head, but I found a bottle of pineapple tequila I had no memory of buying.

"How do you feel about pineapple tequila?" I asked.

"As long as it's tequila, I do not give a fuck," Lark said.

I poured a shot for each of us and brought them back to the couch.

"Bottoms up," I said, and we both tossed our shots back. Lark cringed a little, but she slammed the empty glass down on the coffee table.

"Not bad," she said. "I'd ask for a few more, but I know I have to drive."

The tequila burned just a little bit and I welcomed it. I could definitely use another shot myself.

"Fuck," Lark said with a sigh. She looked toward the TV, and I saw that her eyes were welling up. "It's just bullshit."

"I'm sorry," I said.

She sniffed and I got up to grab her a box of tissues from the bathroom.

"Thanks," she said as I passed it to her. "I hate crying, especially in front of other people. Don't you dare tell anyone about this. I've been taking a shower at Layne's every time I need to cry."

"It's a good place for it," I said as she wiped her eyes and then blew her nose.

"I know I'm being a little bit of an asshole, but I think I'm entitled, given the circumstances," she said. "Everyone has just been so damn nice and it's embarrassing. I feel like all I do is thank people as they give me money and clothes and stuff and offer me anything I could need. I'm so grateful, but I just wish they wouldn't sometimes."

"Life is complicated. You never know how you're going to feel until something happens to you," I said.

"I know I've had a pretty easy life, aside from my mother being awful. Honor cushioned the blow of so many things, sometimes at her own expense. She was willing to get into a loveless marriage to continue to pay for my school. What am I even supposed to do with that?"

From the way she spoke, I could tell she'd been holding onto all of this for a long time. Maybe her whole life.

"Fuck, now I'm rambling. I'm sorry," she said, getting up. "I should go."

"It's okay," I said. Having deep conversations with my hookups was another thing I didn't do, but I was telling myself it didn't count. Lark wasn't a hookup anymore, she was going to be my roommate and my last roommate, Joy, had become one of my best friends. Not that Lark had to step into that role, but being casual friends with her might be okay.

"I'll have the landlord send over the lease and you can just let me know when you want to move in. I'll get you some keys made," I said.

Lark nodded as she edged toward the door.

"Sure, fine," she said. "It'll probably be this weekend."

"Great," I said. "Let me know if you need any help. I'm not going to lift anything heavy, but I'm really good at moving blankets."

Lark's face formed a ghost of a smile. "Good to know."

She started to walk down the stairs and paused. "Thank you, Sydney. For letting me move in. And for the mattress and the other stuff."

"You're welcome," I said. "Joy helped with a lot of it."

"I'll thank her too," she said, and she seemed to want to say something else.

I raised my eyebrows and waited, but then she shook her head.

"I'll see you this weekend," she said.

LARK SIGNED the lease and I got a copy and that was that. She was officially my new roommate. Layne and Honor were acting like I'd done some sort of selfless act, and I had to keep telling them that I was literally desperate for a roommate, and that Lark was the one who was doing me a favor.

She moved in on Saturday, which didn't take that long since most of what she had were clothes and the books Joy had given her. She arranged them on the bookshelf and made the bed with new sheets.

Thankfully the mattress had arrived in time.

"What do you think?" I asked as she sat on it for the first time.

Lark sat up and bounced a little on the bed, reminding me of the bouncing she'd done on my bed.

I looked out the window.

"It's great. Much nicer than the one at the chicken house." When she'd first moved in with Honor, she'd been sleeping on a pullout couch, but she'd moved into Honor's former room.

"Maybe now my back will stop hurting after my shifts," she said.

The air in the room felt too thick, so I backed up until I was out of the room with her. Lark's stuff already had a specific scent that I recognized as distinctively hers. It reminded me of lilies, or some other white flower mixed with a clean, slightly minty scent. In time I'd become used to it and wouldn't even notice anymore.

I needed that time to come sooner rather than later.

Lark was tired from moving, and I could tell she needed

some privacy, so she closed her door and I let her be. Layne had cooked both of us a bunch of food, so the fridge and freezer were full of baking dishes and metal trays. Since Joy had moved out, the quality of my meals had definitely gone down. We'd always promised to split cooking duties, but usually she'd been the one to take over since I could only competently make a few things.

I had no idea what Lark's cooking skills were like and I wasn't going to ask, but I did knock on her door to see if she was hungry.

She answered with puffy eyes and a tired expression.

"Hey, I'm just going to heat up some of that pasta bake Layne made, do you want me to throw some in for you?" I asked.

"I'm not hungry," she said, shaking her head.

Since she was an adult and could decide if she wanted to eat or not, I let it go and she shut her door again.

I heated up the food and ate it in the living room with Clementine, who wouldn't stop running to Lark's door and meowing. Joy had kept her door open most of the time, so he was very confused why this new person was keeping it closed.

"Leave her alone, Clem," I told him. He blinked at me and then meowed loudly and pitifully.

"You're fine, calm down," I said. "Go look at the birds." This was the magic word for Clem. It might be nighttime, but he ran to his little perch in front of the window and jumped up to stare at the birdfeeder that was suction cupped to the other side.

Lark didn't come out for the rest of the night and I went to bed, but I couldn't stop listening for her. The bathroom was right next to my room, so I was aware when she got up and used it. I told myself I was just making sure she was still alive, like any good roommate would.

THAT NIGHT I kept waking up and listening for noises in the apartment. Well, noises other than Clementine doing his nightly zooms through the living room and kitchen.

At last my body gave out and I did get a few hours, but morning came way before I was ready, and even though I hadn't set an alarm, I was awake at my normal work time anyway. On Sundays I liked to sleep in, but that was not meant to be. Maybe I could catch a nap later on the couch.

When I poked my head out of my room, the only one to greet me was Clementine, who immediately screamed to be fed. I padded to the kitchen and opened a can of wet food for him, which he immediately attacked as if he'd never eaten food before.

"Don't eat so fast or else you'll get sick," I told him. He ignored me.

Figuring I might as well be up, I started the coffee and looked in the fridge to see what I could throw together. Layne, angel that she was, had also given us a beautiful mixed veggie quiche, and I was just slicing a piece for myself to warm up when Lark emerged from her room, looking like she hadn't slept much.

"Good morning," I said, and it felt so formal I wished I could take it back.

Lark just grunted and fell into one of the chairs set in front of the counter.

"Do you want some coffee?" I asked. "It's just brewing right now."

Lark nodded. Guess she wasn't a talker in the morning. I could respect that.

"There's quiche too," I said, pointing. "Want some?"

"Sure," Lark said, her voice rough with exhaustion.

I threw two pieces on one plate and stuck it in the

microwave to heat. Lark seemed to just be staring at the countertop.

I wanted to give her space to wake up if she needed it, but I also could not deal with the silence.

"Is, uh, is there anything else you needed to get? We could go shopping if you needed to," I said.

Lark shook her head and the coffee finished filling the pot. She got up and pulled open a few cabinets before finding the coffee mugs. Most of them were rejects that my mom had made.

"There's creamer in the fridge," I said, and she grabbed it, adding just a splash to her cup before sipping it and closing her eyes, as if she'd really needed that.

I heard a phone go off and looked down at mine, but it was silent. Lark walked back to her room to grab her phone and came back out with her thumb typing a response to the message.

I got the quiche out of the microwave and poured my own coffee before I slid Lark her own plate of quiche, along with a fork, all while biting my tongue so I didn't ask her who she was talking to.

"Thanks," she said, still busy on her phone.

She started to eat, and I pretended I was doing something on my phone so I'd stop staring at her. Even without a lot of sleep, she was gorgeous. Seeing her this morning reminded me of that other morning, when I'd woken up before her. Her hair had been spread out on my pillow, her scent had saturated my sheets. Unlike every single other hookup I'd ever had, I had waited to wash them until the day after she'd left and her smell had faded.

"Honor and Layne are just checking in," she finally said, setting her phone down. "They're being extra about it."

"Layne likes to fix everyone's problems," I said.

Lark rolled her eyes. "I wish she'd get another problem to

work on." She sighed and picked at the quiche. "I'm fine," she said, as if she was trying to convince someone.

"Okay," I said.

"I am," she said, as if I'd argued with her.

"Got it," I said, sipping my coffee. I should just go and sit next to her like a normal person, but I ate my quiche standing up with the counter between us.

My original plan for today was to sit on the couch with a pile of books and demolish them and eat a bunch of snacks, but I didn't know if I could do that with Lark around. At least until I got used to her presence and wasn't startled by how pretty she was every time I saw her.

She hadn't even been here for a day and I was already needing a break so I could forget about her, forget about that night, forget about sitting on her face.

"What are you doing today?" Lark asked, pushing her hair out of her face.

"I'm not sure," I said, wondering if she'd just read my mind.

"Do you want to get out of here?" she asked.

I opened my mouth to tell her that I was going to be busy, but the word that came out wasn't what I'd planned. "Sure."

AFTER WE FINISHED BREAKFAST, we each got dressed, shoved our feet into boots, and went downstairs to Lark's car. It wasn't much, even older and rustier than mine, but she assured me it would get us where we needed to go.

"Where are we going?" I asked, wondering how in the hell I'd ended up alone with Lark in her car and knowing it was an extremely bad idea.

"To the movies," she said. "It's warm inside and they have popcorn."

I couldn't argue with that logic.

Lark didn't take us to the usual movie theater that I went to with Layne and Joy to see the latest blockbuster or romance film. We headed onto the highway, and I was dying to ask questions, but kept my mouth shut.

"Do you like classic movies?" Lark asked, pulling into the parking lot of a theater that I'd never been to.

"Depends on the movie," I said. "How classic are we talking?"

"This place shows a lot of old movies in the afternoons on Sunday. Very popular with the older demographic."

She was right; the parking lot was packed.

"What are they showing today?" I asked.

"An absolute classic: *Gaslight*, from 1944. Seen it?" she asked.

"I haven't, but I've heard it's good," I said. Joy and I mostly watched classics that were romances or musicals or both.

"I think you'll like it," Lark said as I followed her through the door. She walked up to the counter and got two tickets and handed over her card before I could protest.

"Consider this a roommate welcome gift," she said. "You've literally given me a bunch of shit lately. I can swing a movie ticket and some snacks."

There wasn't really any arguing with that.

We got popcorn, drinks, and candy. Lark chose the sour Skittles and I selected peanut butter M&M'S.

"You gonna share those?" she asked, nudging me as we headed toward the theater.

"Maybe. I'm an only child, though. Not good about sharing," I said.

"Just going to lean into that stereotype, huh?" she asked as I pushed the door open.

"To justify not having to share my candy? Absolutely," I said.

I let Lark pick where to sit, and she chose the center of a middle row. Fortunately, we'd gotten here early enough that a showing had just let out so we were some of the first people. The downside was that now I had to sit next to Lark and wait for the movie to start.

"Don't you dare eat all that before I've even had some," Lark said, reaching for the popcorn that I had resting on one leg. This theater was old-school and didn't have huge armrests for holding all the snacks and drinks.

"I'm not," I said, even though I'd been shoving popcorn in my face.

Lark snatched the bucket from me and curled herself around it protectively.

"You look like Clementine with his wet food bowl," I said.

Lark just growled at me.

I snorted, unable to not laugh at her.

She did eventually pass the bucket back to me and we opened our candy and shared them back and forth.

"You know, every movie now is like three hours long and they should really build in an intermission so you can get up and pee and get more snacks," Lark said.

"Agree," I said. "I only go to theaters if I really want to see something. As far as I'm concerned, one of the best ways to watch movies is on the big screen that Mark has and lets Layne borrow."

Every summer we'd hang in the pool and watch movies on the big screen. Only downside was they had to be kid-friendly since the twins always wanted to join us if they were around. We saved the more adult content for when they were at camp.

"So weird that your sister wanted to be his second wife," I said.

"Listen, no one has to tell me how fucked up my family is. I've known it my whole life. The second I came out as a lesbian my mom gave up on making me in her image and shifted to

Honor. It's taken a lot of therapy to not feel guilty about that," she said, looking into the bag of sour Skittles as if she was looking for the right flavor. I'd noticed she avoided the orange and yellow ones.

"Sorry," she said, apologizing. "I have a tendency to bring down the mood when I open my mouth sometimes."

"No worries," I said. "I don't mind. You can bring down the mood all you want with me."

Lark looked over at me and we fell into silence. Had I said too much?

"I appreciate that," she said. The lights dimmed and it was time for the movie.

"THE MORAL OF the story is, don't trust your husband," I said as we walked out of the theater. Even though I'd washed my hands in the bathroom, they still had the distinct smell of movie theater butter. I swear, the smell had sunk into my pores.

"Or maybe you shouldn't marry your older music teacher," she said.

"Both can be true," I said.

"I feel like we're throwing both husbands and music teachers under the bus," Lark said, unlocking her car.

"I'm okay with that," I said as I got in.

It was early afternoon and I could tell Lark was a little restless.

"Was there anything else you wanted to do?" I asked.

"Scream," she said, and I couldn't tell if she was joking.

"Go for it," I said.

Lark shook her head. "No, if I'm going to scream, I want to do it somewhere dramatic, like the top of a mountain."

I looked at the exits on the highway and said to keep going when she reached the one to take us back to Arrowbridge.

"Okay, but you're going to have to tell me where we're going," Lark said.

I told her which exit to take, and we drove twenty minutes more until she saw the right town. Once we were off the highway, I directed her through a picturesque tourist town and then into the driveway for a state park with a campground and hiking trails.

"I didn't say I wanted to climb a mountain," Lark said as we got in the line of cars going by the ticket booth.

"We don't have to climb, you can drive up," I said, pointing.

"Oh, good," she said.

We paid our fee and Lark followed the other cars up the steep and winding road that took us up the mountain. It was nice they kept it plowed even in the winter so people could still enjoy going up. I was sure there were some brave souls that hiked in the snow, but it sounded like a bad idea to me.

"I've never been camping," Lark said. "My mother wouldn't stay in anything less than a five-star hotel, and the idea of pissing in the woods might have given her a stroke."

"I'm fine with nature walks and even a hike, but I don't do camping unless I'm staying in a camper that's so nice it might as well be a house. No tents." I shuddered at the thought. I had a little tent I used at the beach to protect my skin from the sun and to give me some privacy when I took beach naps, but that was only for a few hours. I couldn't get comfortable in a tent. I needed room.

"Camping in a camper sounds nice. Some of them are pretty fancy," Lark said, and we reached the summit of the mountain and the tiny parking lot. She parked and we got out and followed other people along a shoveled path to a rock they seemed to be interested in and taking pictures of, and on.

"That's the official top," I told Lark. "I came here a few

times with school. Forcing a bunch of fourth graders to hike a mountain was a terrible idea, but they did it every year."

"My school never did anything like that," she said. "We went to a lot of museums and so forth."

"I would have preferred the museums over the poison ivy rash and twisted ankles," I said.

Lark climbed up on top of the rock and I got out my phone.

"Okay, now pose," I said.

She gave me the finger. "If you take a picture of me, I'll flush your phone."

I slid my phone in my pocket. "Fine. But you said you wanted to scream, so go for it."

Lark stared at me. "The screaming was more metaphorical."

A line had formed of other people who wanted to get a picture of themselves on the official top of the mountain.

"Go ahead, do your scream so these nice people can get their pictures," I said.

Lark looked away and then before I could say anything else, let out an ear-splitting scream. It went on for so long that she used up all her air and was panting as she finished.

A few of the people behind us were bewildered, but Lark just gave me a smile and hopped down to join me.

"Feel better?" I asked.

"Not really, but that was fun," she said. "And now everyone is staring at me."

"Who gives a fuck?" I said.

"Not me," she agreed.

SINCE WE'D PAID and driven all the way up here, we wandered around and found a little shaded area to sit on a

43

raised rock that had a little flat spot like a bench. Lark brushed away the snow and sat down.

"You're an interesting person, Sydney Sparks," Lark said.

"So are you, Lark Conroy," I said, using her full name.

Her stomach growled and I started looking around in my bag for something to eat.

"What the hell do you have in there?" Lark asked as a bunch of things clinked together.

"Lots of stuff," I said, pulling out the snakebite kit and handing it to her. I knew I had a bag of nuts or a granola bar or something.

I pulled out a few paperbacks and handed those to Lark, along with two small bottles of hot sauce.

"You know they make these great things called ebooks and audiobooks now. You can store them in your phone," she said.

"Yeah, yeah, I know. I have plenty of them," I said. "I just like having options. Sometimes my brain doesn't want an ebook."

I pushed aside a packet of seeds and found what I'd been looking for.

"Here you go," I said, handing her the granola bar.

"Oh," she said, handing me back the stuff I'd given her to hold. I tossed it all back in my bag.

"Thanks," she said, opening it and breaking the bar in half.

"No, I'm fine, you have the whole thing," I said.

"If you insist," she said, chomping down on the bar and sighing in relief. I tried not to think about the other types of sighs I'd heard from Lark. In just one night, I had made a whole mental playlist of her noises, and they would start to play in my brain at inopportune times. Like right now.

"So, how was your mountain scream?" I asked.

"Very nice. We should make it into a thing. I feel like there's a way to monetize this and sell it to rich people," she said.

"I mean, they have laughter yoga, so mountain screaming doesn't seem that far off," I said.

"Good point. I'll work on it."

The weather was slightly warm today, but that didn't mean we could sit for too long out in the open without getting chilly, so we were back in the car a few minutes later, our chilly hands pressed to the vents as Lark blasted the heater as high as she could.

"Okay, now I'm ready to be warm inside," she said.

"Back home?" I asked. The home that was mine and hers, and thus ours. Still hadn't wrapped my mind around that yet.

"Yes, please," she said, backing out and getting back onto the road to go back down the mountain.

Chapter Four

"WHY AM I STILL COLD?" Lark asked, banging the snow off her boots and then leaving them in the tray in the doorway.

"I've got a heated blanket somewhere," I said. "Gimme a second."

Now I was kicking myself for not buying one for her at the store when we'd gone shopping. I went into my closet and pulled the heated blanket from the top shelf where it had been folded.

"The only downside is that now Clementine is going to be your best friend," I said. "Hope you don't mind having a fat orange cat in your lap."

"I think I'll manage," she said, taking the blanket and sitting on the couch. That was where I'd wanted to sit, but there definitely wasn't enough room for her to stretch out with the blanket and the cat and for me to sit without touching her.

"Enjoy," I said, feeling awkward. I grabbed my stack of books from the coffee table and shut myself in my room. Reading in bed was just as good as reading on the couch. I put on some music and picked up my first book, but I read the same page three times and then put the book down and grabbed another.

Same situation.

I was usually the kind of person who could completely lose themselves in a book and shut out the world, but it wasn't happening. I sighed and got up. Maybe I just needed some coffee. That would perk me up.

I left my room and saw Lark bundled up in my electric blanket on the couch, the TV playing a movie, and Clementine asleep on her legs.

If she was Joy, I would have asked her if she wanted some coffee too but asking Lark if she wanted coffee seemed...too much. Joy was my best friend. Leaving Lark alone to do her own thing was what regular roommates did.

So I went to the kitchen and started to make coffee and Lark didn't say anything.

"Come on, come on," I said under my breath as the coffee pot took its sweet time. Why was it going so slow?

At last there was enough to fill my cup and I went back to my room as quickly, but as casually as I could and shut the door. Black coffee was fine, so I chugged it down, burning my tongue, and waited for it to kick in before picking up my book again.

This time I was interrupted by a message from Layne, asking how Lark was doing.

She's on the couch watching a movie with Clementine. Seems fine? I sent.

Good. Honor is just a worried little mother hen about her, so I've been tasked with keeping an eye on her via you she responded.

I think Lark needs some space, honestly. She's just trying to figure her shit out and she can't do that when everyone is staring at her and waiting for her to cry or fuck up I sent.

Layne and I had been friends so long that she was used to my bluntness.

I kind of told Honor the same thing, just not that way. I'll see if I can try to get her to back off a bit she replied.

I was writing out a response to Layne when another message came in. This one was from Lark.

Do you mind if I have some of the coffee, or were you going to come get more? she asked.

I shook my head at her texting me when we were literally in the same apartment. Joy would have just yelled from the couch.

Knock yourself out I replied.

I couldn't help but hear her moving from the couch to the kitchen and even the clink of mugs as she grabbed one. Somehow, I was aware of every single move she made in another room. Or maybe I was just hyper aware of her still. Like a low-level sound that I needed to adjust to. She hadn't even lived here for two days. All of this was still new. When Joy had moved in, it had taken us weeks to figure out our routines and who did what chores and a cleaning schedule and so forth.

Lark and I would figure it all out and then I wouldn't hear her every single time she breathed.

FOR THE FIRST time in a long time, it was a relief to go to work. It was a place that didn't smell like Lark. Where I didn't bump into her when I came out of the bathroom. Where I didn't see her after she'd just rolled out of bed. I wasn't exactly a morning person to begin with, and now I had the added complication of seeing a warm and sleepy Lark, her blonde hair glowing in the sunshine that peeked between the curtains. Lark, who always greeted Clementine with enthusiasm, her voice rough from sleep and her eyes puffy and adorable. Seeing someone when they woke up every day was an intimacy that scratched against my skin and made me avoid eye contact with her.

I ate my breakfast with a minimum of conversation and ran down the stairs to unlock the pottery studio fifteen minutes early. Mom was already there, because she practically lived here. At one point she'd pitched the idea of putting a pullout bed in the back, but I'd been able to convince her that was a bad idea.

"Good morning, my baby," she said, kissing me on the cheek the way she did every morning.

"Did you eat?" I asked, as I did every morning.

Mom blinked at me for a second. "Yes?" She didn't sound sure.

"I'll be right back," I said, heading to the café to grab her some breakfast and coffee. Mom would get so into her pottery that she didn't see anything else, and that often included forgetting to eat or drink water. I'd set alarms on her phone for her that went off and prodded her to use the water bottle I'd bought her last Christmas. You'd think being surrounded by so many drinking vessels would remind her, but not so much. It was fine, she was trying.

I got back to the shop and handed the breakfast off to Mom, telling her I'd get to work on opening up for the day. At some point today I needed to head to the post office nearby to send out mug orders. It was my least favorite task, and the one that I couldn't wait to give to someone else when we hired help. I'd given Mom the applications and asked her to look over them, but she had yet to do that. Too busy, she said. Yes, that was the point, I'd thrown back.

I made it to the post office and shipped everything out without too much hassle and the shop was still standing. Mom was actually selling a lamp to a customer when I walked in and

I stood back, letting her go ahead. She was great with certain customers, but not with others. Mom tended to cry if someone's voice got too loud, or if anyone was upset with her, so that didn't really work so great with customer service. That's where I came in.

While I went about my day, doing my little tasks, I couldn't stop thinking about Lark. She was working a shift at the coffee shop today. It was her first one back after the fire. I hoped the customers weren't being nasty to her. Liam would absolutely throw anyone out who abused the baristas, but what if he wasn't around? Was she tired?

Was she thinking about me at all?

"Shit," I said under my breath. This was not a healthy train of thought at all. I was obsessing and I needed to snap out of it.

Technically, I was still on my hookup hiatus. I hadn't been with anyone since that night with Lark. It shouldn't have even happened that night, but she'd caught me in a vulnerable moment, and really, I hadn't needed that much convincing.

No more of that. I needed to stop letting pretty girls seduce me. It came back to bite me on the clit, and not in the fun way.

Work wasn't going to occupy my mind and distract me from Lark, and books hadn't really worked the way they usually did either.

A hobby. I needed a new hobby. A hobby that didn't involve sex.

I need a hobby I sent to both Layne and Joy in our group chat. Honor was also included, but she rarely checked in or responded.

You always say you want to learn to cook Joy said.

No I replied.

Well, we have lots of craft books at the bookstore. Let me know if you want me to grab you some Joy said.

I'm looking up a list of hobbies Layne said. **A lot of them involve art**

No I replied again. **No art. You know I can't do anything like that.** I hated even thinking about just how bad I was at art. Various people had told me over my life that if only I practiced, I'd get better at art, but every time I tried to paint or draw, it always came out like absolute shit and it felt like shit, and I was miserable. Why would I keep doing something that made me miserable? So I stopped trying until I'd graduated from college and had moved back to Arrowbridge because I didn't have any other options. My marketing degree was shiny and new, but I hadn't counted on all of the connections I was supposed to have been making so I could secure a decent job or even an internship. Missed that lecture, apparently.

I'd come back to Arrowbridge and had started working in the shop and Mom had given up on forcing me to ruin the name of pottery after only a week. At that time, she was still selling her work out of the garage. I'd been the one to tell her that she needed an actual storefront and had been the one to negotiate the original rental agreement for this place.

I didn't even know how I'd done it. Fresh out of college, and I'd been pretty much in charge of everything. A lot of caffeine and confidence had been involved. Now I was much world-wearier and wiser, and I hoped I'd never have to do it again.

Got it. No art. What about dancing, or yoga? You know McKenna would help Joy sent.

McKenna would teach me how to do yoga, but that didn't call to me.

I don't know. If you have any more ideas, please send them my way I added and then went back to work.

LARK MESSAGED me to let me know when she was on her way back from the coffee shop and asked if I wanted her to pick up dinner. I told her that was fine, and I was flexible with whatever she wanted to get.

Tacos? she asked.

Perfect I replied and pulled out my hot sauce to prepare in case she didn't grab any to go with it.

I read while I waited, our new book club book. It was affectionately known as "the MILF book," due to it being a romance between a woman and her daughter's best friend, and so far, it was scorching hot.

Clementine announced Lark's arrival before I heard her walk through the door with a bag of tacos.

"Dinner is served," she said as she slid her boots off and removed her winter coat.

"Not for kitties," she said to Clementine.

"He just ate," I said as Clementine rolled onto his back and meowed pitifully.

"Are you sure? He disagrees with you," Lark said, carefully rubbing his belly and taking her hand away before he could attack it.

"He's a little furry liar," I said, looking down at my cat. He blinked innocently.

Lark started pulling tacos out.

"I got a little bit of everything," she said.

I pulled out some plates and looked through, grabbing two beef crunchy tacos, some rice and beans, and some queso to top it with.

"Hot sauce?" I asked.

"They just had the little packets and I know you have a more discerning palate," she said. "So I didn't get it."

I was an "any hot sauce port in a taco storm" usually, but I liked that she'd thought about me when making the decision.

"That works," I said, opening the bottle and shaking it over everything. "Want some?" She shook her head at the offered bottle.

"I'm good."

We took our plates to the living room and sat together on the couch.

"Um, did you want to watch anything?" Joy and I usually put on an episode of a reality show or something when we had dinner. Nothing that we had to think too much about and could talk over.

"Oh, sure," she said. "I'm fine with whatever."

I went to the baking show that I liked to watch with Joy sometimes. There was a new episode, but it seemed rude to put that on if she hadn't seen the whole season, so I went back to the beginning.

"I've been meaning to watch this, but I haven't yet," she said. "Isn't there a queer woman on this season?"

"Yup, and she's hot as hell," I said. "I don't even care if she can bake. She should just win by default."

Not wanting to spoil the rest of the season, I didn't tell Lark that the woman I was rooting for was in the semi-final and I couldn't wait to see if she was going to win.

The show was sweet and low-stress, perfect after a long day. My tacos weren't great, but they were good enough and I finished my plate before going back to see if there was anything left. I added two soft tacos to my plate and dressed them with hot sauce before sitting down with Lark again. She seemed to be fixated on the show, so that gave me a chance to watch her.

I still wasn't used to how sexy she was, and it seemed like she was only getting hotter by the minute. A soft smile played on her face as she watched the contestants get introduced.

"I've always wanted to know how to bake," she said. "But it seems so difficult."

"I know. I tried to make bread once and it was a complete

disaster. Just awful." I shuddered at the memory. That was when Joy had patted my shoulder and told me we should just get bread from the grocery store.

"Too bad Christmas has already passed. I could have asked Honor for a bread machine."

"You could ask her now. I'm sure she'd get you one," I said.

Lark set down her empty plate. "True. I feel like I could get away with murder right now. Have anyone you want to off?"

She turned and faced me instead of the TV screen.

"I'd have to think about that," I said, finishing my last taco. "Can I get back to you?"

"Just hurry, because I don't know how long this 'oh poor fire girl' thing is going to last."

"Got it," I said.

Silence fell between us and I didn't know what to do with it, so I got up to deal with my dish.

Lark followed me with hers, and I tossed the remnants of the tacos and loaded my plate into the dishwasher.

"Are we not going to talk about it?" Lark asked quietly.

"Talk about what?" I asked.

"You know what about," she said, crossing her arms and leaning on the counter. She was blocking the way back into the living room, so I was trapped.

"I just assumed you didn't want to talk about it," I said. "You hadn't said anything."

"I know, but I think we should, since we're living together now."

I closed my eyes. "Then I'm going to need some more pineapple tequila."

THIS TIME neither of us needed to drive, so after downing one shot, I immediately poured both of us another.

"Can we sit down for this?" I asked. Lark went to the couch with the shot glasses, and I followed her with the bottle.

"Give me a second." I needed the alcohol to kick in first.

Lark waited and petted Clementine in the meantime.

"Just one more," I said, pouring myself a third shot I knew I was probably going to regret tomorrow morning, but threw back anyway. Lark watched me, not going for her third.

"Okay," I said, feeling the fire starting to glow in my belly. "Go for it."

Lark looked at me.

"You're the one who wanted to talk about it. So talk," I said.

Lark rolled her eyes. "I'm not going to force this on you, Sydney. If you don't want to be mature, then fine. But I'm enough of an adult to sit down and discuss things rationally."

Ouch. That stung, but I wasn't going to let her know that.

"I'm mature," I said, but we both knew that wasn't true.

"We don't have to make this into a big deal. It was just a hookup. But I'm not going to walk around like it didn't happen," Lark said.

"I'm not walking around like it didn't happen. I'm acting like it didn't affect my life because it didn't. None of my hookups do. That's the point."

I'd said words like that so many times, but this was the first time they felt...wrong.

Lark poured herself another shot and tossed it back, slamming the glass down.

"Fine. Works for me. See? That wasn't so bad."

She got up from the couch and went to her room and slammed the door.

What the fuck just happened?

LARK DIDN'T COME out of her room for the rest of the night, but I did hear her go to the bathroom and take a shower before going into the kitchen and getting something. She spoke softly to Clementine, who meowed back at her. I waited until I heard her door close before I ventured out and went to grab water for myself. The alcohol had worn off, leaving me parched and irritated.

I downed two glasses of water and grabbed a bag of chips to munch as I read. The book club book was getting spicy again, and it was actually keeping my attention, which was nice.

I tiptoed toward Lark's door and listened, but there was no sound from the other side. She'd probably gone to bed. Clementine meowed and I tried to shush him before running back to my room and closing the door again.

Chapter Five

LARK AVOIDED me for the rest of the week, which was fine, because I was avoiding her too. When we did end up both out of our rooms in the apartment, she didn't say anything to me. Clementine got lots of affection, which he appreciated.

This was pretty much what I'd wanted in a roommate. She did her thing, I did mine, and we respected each other's space.

Why the fuck was I completely miserable?

"What is up with you lately?" Layne asked me as we lounged in her living room on Sunday. I'd been desperate to get out of my apartment and see my two best friends, so Layne had invited me and Joy over, and Honor was taking Lark clothes shopping again. I wasn't sure Lark wanted more clothes, but that didn't exactly matter to Honor. More clothes Lark would get.

"Nothing," I said as she passed me a cup of hot chocolate she'd made. I took a sip. "Holy fuck, this is good."

Layne leaned down and stage-whispered "the secret is heavy cream and vanilla."

"Good to know," I said, as if I was ever going to actually make this. My usual hot cocoa came powdered.

"But back to your mood," Layne said, and I frowned, wishing she'd drop it. "Are things not working out well with Lark?"

"Things are fine with Lark," I said. "I'm fine."

Layne and Joy shared a look, and I wished my best friends weren't such empathetic people. It made my life difficult.

"You've been using the f word a lot lately," Joy said gently. I hated that tone of her voice. I knew what it meant. Joy and Layne had been talking about me behind my back.

"Well, I wouldn't have to use it so much if you would just believe me and stop asking me how I'm doing," I said, getting up from the couch. I didn't know where I was going, so I ended up in the kitchen, pacing around in a circle.

"If you want us to leave you alone, just say so. If you want to actually talk about it, then we're good with that too," Layne said. She and Joy had stayed in the living room, giving me space.

"I want you to leave me alone," I said, enunciating the words. "I mean, I don't want you to ignore me, but I want you to stop worry about me, fuck. Nothing is wrong with me, Lark and I are adjusting to living together, the world is still spinning. Okay?"

My voice had gotten loud and I realized I'd been yelling. *Good job, Syd.*

"I'm sorry. I'm just tired," I said, rubbing my itchy eyes. I had been having issues sleeping lately. I just couldn't get comfortable when it was time to sleep. Work was still draining, and I was just feeling stretched way too thin, even without the Lark situation. Which wasn't even a situation. It was a big bowl of nothing.

Layne and Joy shared another look and both nodded.

"Okay then," Layne said, taking a breath. "If you don't want to talk about that, I need both of you to help me because I think Honor wants to get married sooner rather than later."

That was a hell of a subject change.

"Holy shit," I said, coming back into the living room. "Tell me."

WHEN I GOT BACK to the apartment, there were a bunch of bags in the way of the door. I carefully pushed them aside so I could take off my boots.

"Lark?" I said, saying her name out loud for the first time in days.

"What?" A tired voice said from the couch. From this angle I couldn't see her. She sat up and looked at me.

"Sorry about the mess."

"It's okay," I said, trying not to trip over the bags. "I've always been fine with being an only child, but now I'm kind of wishing I had a sister."

"You can have mine," she said.

Since we were actually speaking, I went to sit on the couch. Lark moved so I'd have room.

"She doesn't listen to me. When I was younger, I used to think there was an age I'd get to where she'd actually hear me when I told her what I wanted or didn't want. I thought it had happened when I dropped out of school, but here we are." She gestured at the bags. "There's a bunch of stuff in here. Take whatever you want."

Lark and I were almost the same height, but her body was curvier than mine, so I wasn't sure what she'd bought would fit or look good on me, but I was still going to look.

"I'm sorry," I said.

"Not your problem," she said, leaning back to look at the ceiling.

"I know Layne was going to talk to her about letting up," I said.

"I'm sure my sister got distracted by boobs and didn't hear anything," she said, and I couldn't help but snort with laughter.

"Boobs are distracting," I said, forcing myself to my eyes on her face and not look at that part of her anatomy. "She'll calm down, I'm sure," I said, trying to be nice. "And if not, I'll give you a shopping list next time."

"Thanks," she said with a sigh. "Liam asked me to go full-time at the coffee shop." She said it softly.

"That's great," I said, and she nodded.

"I know. It really is. Being a full-time barista is such a joke to so many people, but I fought for this job. I work really fucking hard and I'm proud of myself," she said, daring anyone to disagree with her.

"You should be proud of yourself. Do you know how many people would have a breakdown after just one shift as a barista?" I said.

Lark nodded and picked at the knee of her jeans.

"I know," she said. "It's not a dream career, but it's some-thing, and it's mine."

"Managing my mom's pottery shop was my backup backup backup plan," I said. "I only did it because she was struggling and I couldn't get hired anywhere here, in spite of knowing everyone who was hiring. It was brutal."

I shuddered. Nothing could make me want to go back to those first few months after college when I was in constant panic mode about the state of my life. Sure, the shop wasn't my dream, and I didn't want to spend my life there, but it was a steady paycheck, and it was pretty much the same every day. I could pretty much go through my day on autopilot. The only problem with that is some days I was bored out of my fucking mind and considered smashing every single piece of pottery so I wouldn't have to sell any of it.

"I still have no idea what I want to do. I've taken every single personality test and job test and they all give me different answers. It's probably a bad sign that I'm not passionate about anything," she said.

"I'm passionate about my bills getting paid. That's about it," I said, and Lark chuckled.

"I get that."

This seemed like a conversation that needed tea, so I got up and filled the kettle, like I would have done if I'd been having this conversation with Joy.

"Are you okay with lemon ginger tea?" I asked.

"Yeah," Lark said.

I brought her a cup and she took it from me gently. "Thanks."

Having a cup of tea in your hands was a good distraction when talking about deep topics.

"What do you want to do?" Lark asked.

"Read books all day," I said. "Sometimes when the shop is slow, I'll put on an audiobook. When the bookstore opened, I thought about applying, but I don't want to sell books. I just want to read them."

Lark nodded. "I like reading too. And sleeping. Big fan."

"Fuck, I love a good nap," I said. "And a good bath."

Lark nodded. "Totally."

"I have a degree in marketing, so sometimes I think about doing something with that, but I never get very far. Of course, I could start my own company and be a freelancer, but that's a complete gamble," I said.

Lark nodded. "Yeah, I get it. I've thought about all kinds of things, but they all seem too unstable. With the coffee shop, I know exactly what I'm getting based on the hours I worked. It might not be as much as I'd like, but I can set a budget. Free-lancing is rolling the dice."

I nodded. It was a dilemma.

"Sometimes I think I'm too practical when it comes to

careers, which is funny, because no one who knows me would say I was practical," I said.

"Practical people are boring. Look at my sister."

"Honor isn't boring. She's just too tightly wound. Less tight now that she's with Layne," I said.

Lark conceded that point. "That's true. She does smile and laugh a lot more. And she isn't up my ass all the time. I should thank Layne."

We finished our tea and talked about career options, but we didn't get anywhere. The show was completely forgotten.

"Okay, enough work talk. I need to read something dirty," she said.

"If you need any recommendations, I am happy to offer them. And you can borrow any of my books that you want."

I didn't lend my books to just anybody, but Lark was different. She'd been through a lot and I just…wanted to be nice to her. She'd dealt with a lot of shit in her life, more shit than some people. Lark deserved softness.

"Thanks," she said. "I'm still working on the ones that Joy got for me. That was really sweet of her."

"She's the best," I said.

"Sorry I'm a roommate downgrade," she said.

"You're not," I said, nudging her with my foot. "And the bar was really, really high. There's only one Joy Greene and I lost custody of her to Ezra."

"I lost my sister to Layne, but honestly, I was fine with that. She can have her."

She laughed and I knew Honor wouldn't have taken that comment personally at all and would have said the same thing about Lark if the roles were reversed.

"I think Layne's very happy with their arrangement," I said.

"So's Honor. The walls between their bedroom and the

living room are very thin," Lark said with a shudder. "Layne's loud."

I snorted. "I'm sure. I've never been particularly quiet myself. Poor Joy had to invest in earplugs and noise-canceling headphones."

"She should have left them for me," Lark said. "Or are you still on your hiatus?"

Shit. I shouldn't have brought up the headphones. Now we were talking about my sex life. Normally it was a perfectly fine topic of conversation for me, but not with Lark.

"Still on hiatus," I said.

"Because of me?" she asked. How the hell had we come back around to this again? It was like Lark had deliberately steered us in this direction even after I'd said I didn't want to talk about it anymore.

"No," I said, and I could hear the defensiveness in my voice. "You were a blip in the hiatus, and I went right back to it and things are going great."

"Okay, sure," she said, smirking a little bit.

"I'm going to read," I announced, standing up from the couch.

"Sounds like a plan," Lark said, still smiling and unbothered.

I really wanted to argue with her, but I also wanted to flee, so I chose the second option and shut myself in my room with a pile of books.

LATER ON THAT night I left my room to go take a shower. I tried to let the hot water soothe the tension from my body, but it wasn't working. So far, I hadn't gotten desensitized to Lark. If anything, I was more and more aware of her with each day that passed. I ran my hand down my belly and slid it between my legs.

The other side effect of Lark Awareness was being constantly horny. It distracted me at work, when I came home, when I was trying to sleep, all the time.

I hadn't snuck my mini waterproof vibe in with me, but right now I didn't need it. My hands had years of experience and knew what they were doing. Slickness that had nothing to do with the water from the showerhead ran down my leg as I circled my clit before sliding two fingers inside to press at my g-spot, then back out to tease my clit again. The other hand was hard at work pulling and pinching my nipples and before I had prepared myself, an orgasm crashed through my body, causing me to lean up against the shower wall for support as my body gave itself over to pleasure.

I stepped back under the water and went on with my shower routine, even though I could have come again easily. If I needed to come again to get to sleep, I could do it in bed with one of my toys.

I left the bathroom wrapped in my bath sheet and listened for Lark. Nothing. Being as quiet as I could, I crept over to her door and listened. Nothing. I was just about to leave when her door opened, and I fell right into a warm body.

"Fuck!" I yelled at the same time as she screeched. The two of us almost fell to the ground, but somehow she had enough presence of mind to keep both of us upright.

In the chaos, my towel slipped and landed in a heap on the floor.

"Shit," I said, leaning down to snatch it up and cover myself, even though she'd seen me naked already.

"What the hell are you doing?" Lark asked, her entire face red as I fumbled to cover myself.

"Nothing," I said, looking down to make sure my boobs

weren't hanging out as I dripped on the floor. "I was just... I was checking on you?" It sounded like a question.

"Okay," she said, unsure as she stepped around me. "You don't need to. I'm fine." How many times had I said those exact words?

"Yeah, sorry," I said, finally meeting her eyes. Her face was still red, and she was breathing a little heavily. I didn't miss the way her eyes flicked up and down my body.

I had an impulse and did it without thinking: I dropped the towel.

"What are you doing?" Lark asked, her eyes going wide.

"Oops," I said.

Before I knew what was happening, Lark was pushing me up against the wall and her mouth crashed over mine.

I let out a little gasp that she swallowed as she kissed me, her entire body shaking as if she'd been holding herself back. Lark didn't seem to mind that I was still wet from the shower as her hands grabbed at my skin and she tried to pull me closer as I grasped at her clothes.

Just as I was pulling at her shirt, she stepped backwards.

"I'm sorry," she said, putting her hand to her mouth. "I'm sorry."

"What are you sorry for?" I asked.

Lark closed her eyes, as if she couldn't look at me anymore. "We shouldn't."

On some level, I knew she was right, but right now I was too horny, and she was too sexy to care.

"Please, Syd," she said softly.

"Okay, fine," I said, picking up my towel. "I'm covered again."

She squinted her eyes open and then went to the bathroom without another word. I stood there in a puddle and tried to get my shit together to go back to my room.

LARK DIDN'T SAY anything about the kiss the next morning, and I didn't bring it up either. There was definitely an awkwardness between us, so I escaped to the pottery shop as quickly as I could, so I didn't have to be with her. This was her first week full-time at the coffee shop, and I wanted to wish her good luck, but I just kept my mouth shut.

"I have so much to do before book club," Joy said as we ate our usual Monday lunch.

"Do you need any help?" I asked. She usually didn't ask and wanted to do everything on her own.

"Yes, please," she said, and I was surprised. "If you could pick up the cake on Thursday during lunch, and come a little early to help me set up?"

"Sure I can. I bet Lark would want to help too." She was a newer member, but still, I knew she looked forward to it every month.

"That would be great," Joy said. "And I know that Layne hasn't proposed to Honor yet, but I'm already planning a party for them."

Of course she was.

"Let me guess, brownies will feature prominently?" I asked.

"I already reached out to Sweet's and asked if they're up for making custom brownies. They're just waiting for me to give them the green light," Joy said.

"You really are a good friend, Joy," I said. "It makes the rest of us look bad."

She smiled and ate the rest of her cobb salad.

"Give yourself a little bit of credit," Joy said.

"You're right, I'm amazing," I said, and she laughed.

Chapter Six

THAT NIGHT I was feeling comfort food, so I made my favorite potsticker soup. It was something I always made when I had a shitty day, or I was under the weather, but it seemed like something Lark might like. I was just slicing the scallions when she came through the door.

"Hey," she said, taking off her boots and coat.

"Hey," I said. "I'm making soup if you want some."

She paused for a second, her eyes flicking toward her door as if she was going to bolt.

Clementine ran over from his spot at the window observing the bird situation to come say hello to her.

"Sure," she said at last, and I pulled out a bowl for her.

"How was work?" I asked, trying to keep things normal.

"Long," she said, sliding onto one of the chairs and resting her elbow on the counter. "Do you know Mia Davidson?"

"Yeah, I do," I said. Mia had been several years behind me in school, so we hadn't really hung out. She'd gone off to college and I had heard she'd moved back to Arrowbridge but hadn't known what she was doing.

"I told her I was living with you and she said to say hello. She and I work a lot together at the coffee shop."

"Well tell her I said hello back," I said, ladling soup into two bowls and putting a spoon into the one for Lark before sliding it over to her.

"Thanks," she said. "This looks really good."

"It's just soup," I said, getting my bowl and joining her at the counter.

"It's better than a frozen dinner," she said.

"I don't know, those frozen dinners are really good," I said. "I remember I used to beg my mom to get them when I was a kid and she never would, but then I finally had one and it was so gross. I was really disappointed."

"My mom never let us have that kind of thing either," Lark said. "Then I went to college and it was all I ate for a while. I went wild and ate all the things that would have pissed her off in like the first month of school. Got it out of my system. The funny thing was, even if I'd sent her a picture of all of it, she probably wouldn't have cared."

Lark cut one of the potstickers with her spoon.

"I know I've said this before, but your mom really is a piece of work," I said, shaking my head.

"Believe me, I know," she said.

"What about your dad?" I asked. Neither Honor or Lark had ever mentioned a father.

Lark shrugged. "He was one of Mom's many rich husbands and he's dead now. I barely even remember him. Can't mourn someone you didn't know in the first place."

I didn't think that was quite true. I hadn't had a father in my life either, but I'd felt his absence for years. Every time I saw another girl with her dad, I had a sick jealous feeling in my stomach. That feeling lessened as I'd gotten older, but it would still randomly pop up sometimes.

"Oh, I meant to ask you if you could help set up book club on Thursday. No pressure, but I thought I'd ask," I said.

"Yeah, sure. Just let me know when to be there," she said.

"Will do," I said and then we went back to our respective bowls of soup in silence.

Clementine meowed and I realized I'd forgotten to give him dinner, so I filled his bowl.

Lark finished her soup and went back for seconds, which was flattering. Guess she liked it.

"I think I'm going to try and learn how to cook. Layne said she'd help me," Lark said. "I'm kind of lacking in life skills and I don't want to feel like I don't know what the fuck I'm doing."

I got another bowl of soup even though I didn't want it, just so I'd have an excuse to sit down next to her again.

"I don't know if anyone ever feels like they know what the fuck they're doing. I sure don't," I said. I'd just kind of accepted the fact that I would never feel like a competent adult. My friends who all seemed competent said they felt the same way. Well, maybe not Honor, but she was an outlier and couldn't be counted with the general population.

"Well, I'm going to try and figure my shit out. We're starting with breakfast," she said.

"Makes sense," I said, cutting a potsticker into small pieces. "I've always bought frozen waffles, but if you get really good at making them, then we should get a waffle iron."

The moment I mentioned it, an image of Lark making waffles wearing an apron and nothing else flitted through my mind.

I really had to stop doing that. The image didn't go away, it just morphed into Lark making waffles and me joining her in the kitchen, putting my arms around her from behind, and nuzzling the back of her neck as sunlight poured through the apartment and Clementine wrapping himself around our legs.

It was no less sexy, but it was…intimate. Way too intimate. I cut off the thought like slamming a book shut.

"You okay?" Lark said.

"Yeah," I said. "Just drifted off for a second there. What are you and Layne going to make first?"

"I think we're starting with eggs. I love poached eggs, but I have literally no idea how to make them," she said.

"Yeah, me neither. I know it involves dropping the eggs into water, but that just seems like a recipe for egg soup." I shuddered at the idea. Egg drop soup was delicious but just eggs in water? Yuck.

"I'm going to find out," Lark said, her voice full of determination.

"Good for you. Make those eggs your bitch," I said.

She snorted into her bowl. "Bitch Eggs sounds like a feminist punk band."

"Love it. If I could carry a tune at all, I'd love to join that band."

Lark set her spoon down. "I can sing. A little."

"You can?"

She shrugged. "I mean, I'm not winning a Grammy, but yeah. I can carry a tune if I want."

I pushed my soup aside and turned in my seat. "Can I hear a little something?"

Lark blushed a little and shook her head. "Not right now. I'd have to warm up my voice."

"I'd like to hear you, even if it's rough," I said. There was nothing more in this world that I'd like to hear than Lark's singing voice.

Lark rolled her eyes. "Okay, fine. But you can't look at me."

I sighed and turned my back to her.

She inhaled and started to sing. My mouth dropped open within the first two seconds.

Lark had been selling herself short. Her voice was unbelievable. As she continued the song, her voice got stronger and she let it out, filling the entire apartment with the rich sound. I didn't know shit about music, but I knew that she was good. Damn good.

I also knew she was good because I hadn't even recognized the song at first as an upbeat pop song that she'd somehow transformed into a melancholy ballad that almost made you want to cry.

I couldn't see her face as she sang and I wished I could, but I'd agreed not to look at her.

At last, the song faded and she held the last note and was silent. I had to remind myself how to breathe as I'd been too invested in her song to bother.

"Can I turn around now?" I asked, my voice shaky.

"Yeah," Lark said quietly.

I turned around in my seat and before she could say or do anything, I leaned forward and kissed her. Lark let out a little sound of surprise before she hesitated for a second and kissed me back.

Realizing I should not be kissing her, I pulled away.

"Sorry," I said. "I don't even know what that was."

Lark studied me for a second, her cheeks flushed so prettily I had to grip the chair so I didn't reach for her instead.

"It's fine," she said, and then hopped off the chair, taking her bowl to the dishwasher. As soon as that was done, she headed for her room and shut the door.

I guess we weren't going to talk about this either.

LARK'S SINGING voice echoed through my head for the rest of the night and through the next day. Every time I tried to tell her what a good singer she was, though, the words stuck in my throat and I couldn't come up with a casual way to tell her. I had never had an issue like that before and I didn't like it one bit. I'd never been so tongue-tied or worked up around a girl before and it needed to stop.

I told Joy that I need to talk with her and Layne after book club and that it was a friend emergency.

"Oh, that sounds serious," Joy said when I dropped off the cake for book club later and she put it in the fridge.

"Yeah, I'm having…issues," I said. I didn't want to get into it now, but I was in desperate need for advice from the two people I trusted the most.

"I'm here for you, babe," she said, giving me a hug. Joy's hugs could cure almost anything. She rubbed my back and let me go with a supportive smile.

"I'm fine, Joy. I'm not dying or anything, so don't get too worked up," I said.

"You're my best friend. Of course I'm going to get worked up over you," she said, rubbing my arm.

"Likewise," I said. "Everything good with Ezra?"

If Joy ever told me that things weren't good, or that she needed to come back, I would be there in a second.

"Yeah, everything is good," she said with a beaming smile that made her eyes sparkle. "I finally, finally got her to go to therapy to deal with some things, and she's going to apply to schools for the fall so she can finally get her Masters and become a sex therapist."

It had taken a long time for Ezra to reveal to me and Layne that she worked as a sex advice columnist and sex toy reviewer with the dream to become a sex therapist. Honestly, I found it all fascinating and wished she'd talk more about her work. I wanted to know if my theory about every single human being into at least one "weird" (by society's standards) sex thing was correct.

"That's so great," I said. "I wish I could send some of my old hookups her way." I shuddered. Even though I was selective with who I slept with, every now and then I'd get surprised, and not in a good way. There had definitely been more good than bad, but the bad definitely stood out in my memories.

"Yeah, I don't need to know about that," Joy said. "Ezra might, I definitely don't."

I wished that I could just talk to her now and magically conjure Layne, but our talk would have to wait.

"Thanks so much for getting the cake," Joy said, giving me another hug as if sensing I needed one for the road.

"I'll be by later to help," I said.

"With Lark, right?" Joy said, filling her voice with suggestion.

"Yeah, she'll be here. I think," I said, trying to keep my tone casual.

"Well, I'll see you *both* later," Joy said with a wink.

"Yeah, sure, fine," I said as I left.

I WAS BACK at Mainely Books only a few hours later after I'd closed the pottery shop down for the day. Joy was running around when I got there, stressed out as usual. She'd been doing book club for almost as long as the bookshop had been open, but she had a little panic every single month, as if things weren't going to come together.

I was curious how people were going to respond to this month's book, since it was pretty sexy. Our club was a range of people, some who liked spicier books than others.

I'd adored the book and thought it had just the right amount of banging in it, which was on nearly every page.

For next month's pick, my top two choices were an absolutely heart-wrenching lyrical young adult book about a girl who wants to travel to space that I'd already read once, and a contemporary romance set in New York that involved a bar, rescue kittens, and a reality show that I hadn't read yet. If I could, I was going to try and sway the group toward my choices, even though we all voted anonymously via email.

"What can I do?" I asked Joy.

"Set up the snacks," she told me as she rushed to hang up the twinkly lights, hopping on a chair.

"What did I tell you about climbing on chairs?" Ezra said as she came in from the back with a box of stuff. She went right over to Joy, picked her up, and deposited her on the floor again.

"Let me do it."

Ezra used a stepstool to string the lights as Joy supervised and directed her.

I was just setting out some chips when someone tapped me on the shoulder.

"Hey," Lark said, holding a plate of pastries. "I brought these from work."

"Wow, thanks," I said, my voice just a little too cheerful. "If you want to just put them here."

Lark set the pastries down. "Um, so what else can I help with?"

"Well, Joy didn't ask me to get the drinks set up, but they're not, so I'm going to guess that needs to be done too," I said.

Lark followed me back to the fridge where we grabbed everything, including wine for those who wanted it. Ezra had brought the glasses out in the box, so Lark and I put everything out, probably being a little too extra with the arrangement, but it was fun.

Joy and Ezra finally got the lights up and started arranging the chairs.

Before we knew it, people were arriving, bringing even

more snacks. Some of these people I only saw once a month, and it was good to catch up. I hoped Lark didn't feel like I was abandoning her, but she perked up when Layne and Honor arrived together. She might say that her sister annoyed her, but the two of them were tight. They'd united against the tyranny of their mother and had had to raise themselves without her help. For all her faults, my mother did make sure that I made it into adulthood knowing how to cook at least a few things, clean, do laundry, pay bills, and generally care for myself. Honor and Lark's mother had taught classes in Manipulating Men 101 and How to Get the Most Out of Your Alimony 203. If one day Lark told me that her mom taught her how to give a great blowjob, I would not have been surprised.

At last, it was time to start and we all took our seats with snacks and drinks and Joy got ready to lead. She was a little nervous every time, but once she got going, she was a great moderator. I had never been in another book club, but this one was extremely lowkey, which was one of the reasons I loved it.

"Can we talk about the sex scenes? I'm gonna talk about the sex scenes," I said, when Joy asked anyone if they wanted to talk about their favorite parts.

I felt several people roll their eyes. I always talked about the sex scenes.

A few members fell silent when I started talking, but Ezra shared as well, and we had a good discussion about sex scenes in sapphic romance specifically.

Lark usually shared her opinions, but tonight she was pretty quiet. Still, I did catch her glancing at me a few times, and I felt myself blush in response, which made me want to hide under my chair. I wasn't a person who blushed.

Everyone had cake and we chatted about the next book and I put in my points about my two favorites, but we'd see what the consensus was.

"Do you need any help cleaning up?" Lark asked as she hung around.

"No, we've got this," I told her. "I'll see you upstairs."

"Oh," she said, her face falling. "Okay."

"I'll be up later," I said, wondering why she seemed upset. Lark left and it was just me, Layne, Honor, Joy, and Ezra.

"I'm sorry, but I need them," I said, grabbing Joy and Layne's arms. "I'll give them back, but I need them right now."

I dragged them off to the storage room and shut the door.

"I have a problem with Lark," I said.

"YES, we know, and I have some bad news for you, babe," Joy said, trying to hold back a smile. "But I think you have feelings for Lark."

I scoffed. "No. No way. What makes you think that?"

Layne and Joy shared a look.

"It's pretty obvious," Joy said.

"Syd?" Layne said, putting her hand on my arm. "I know your whole thing is being anti-feelings, but that doesn't work in reality. And it's not a bad thing. Feelings are good," she said.

I narrowed my eyes. "Feelings are bad. I don't want them. I don't need them."

"You have feelings for us," Joy said.

"Yeah, friendship feelings. That's different," I said.

I crossed my arms and leaned back in my chair.

"You can't control being attracted to someone," Joy said gently.

"Attraction is fine. I'm attracted to lots of women. It's the other stuff," I said, cringing and squirming in my seat. I'd wanted this conversation but now all I wanted to do was get out of it.

"The emotions?" Layne said. "Kind of overwhelming, aren't they?"

Layne and Joy shared a look of two people who knew a secret.

"I mean...no. Yes. I don't know," I mumbled.

When Lark had sung and I'd kissed her, that had been overwhelming. If I was honest, everything about that first night and the next morning had been, too. Not to mention the thing with me dropping my towel.

"I mean, just because I can hear her breathe when she's in the living room and sometimes I get up in the middle of the night and stand outside her door to make sure she's okay, doesn't mean I care about her," I said.

"Did you hear the words that just came out of your mouth?" Layne just asked. "Because I did."

"I heard them too," Joy said, raising her hand.

I glared at both of them. "I'm regretting having this talk now."

"It's not our fault you like her," Layne said.

"You *really* like her," Joy said, her voice full of glee. She'd been predicting that I would fall for someone for years now.

"Fuck you, no I don't," I said, standing up, but unsure of where to go. If I went upstairs, I'd be confronted by Lark and I was feeling a little vulnerable right now. This conversation had exposed my raw underbelly in ways that I didn't like. I hated being vulnerable so much.

"You're allowed to like someone," Layne said gently. "And you could do worse than liking Lark. She's great, Syd."

"Yes, we both approve. Not that you need our approval, but we both like her," Joy added.

"This is my nightmare," I said, closing my eyes. I could feel my body starting to sweat.

"Our baby is all grown up and falling for someone," Layne said, beaming as she looked at Joy as if this was the best day.

"I hate both of you," I said.

"No you don't, you love us," Layne said, coming over to give me a hug. I growled at her as Joy wrapped her arms around me too.

"I don't like it," I said.

"We know, babe. We know," Joy said, stroking my hair.

Chapter Seven

SOMEHOW, I was able to get them off the topic of Lark and we talked about other random things, including Layne's proposal ideas for Honor.

"She will murder me if we do it in public, but I know she's going to want something elaborate," Layne said. "I don't do elaborate. I've looked up proposal ideas online and so many of them seem so expensive or time consuming."

"Are you sure she wants elaborate?" Joy said. "I know she's a very classy woman, but she loves you and I think she just wants something that's from the heart."

"I don't know. It's stressing me out," Layne said. "I'm so excited, but I just want it to be perfect for her."

"It will be," Joy said. "You'll figure it out."

"Just give it to her during sex. Then she won't say no," I said, and they both looked at me. "What? It's true."

"I'm not doing a mid-coitus proposal, Syd," Layne said. "But that's a good idea for you."

I shuddered. "Absolutely not. No way I'm getting anywhere near marriage." It was absolutely fine and lovely for other people, but it was a hell no from me. Never, never, ever. Nope.

"We'll see," Joy sang, and I glared at her again.

I BRACED myself walking back into the apartment, but Lark wasn't in the living room when I shut the door. I heard the water running in the bathroom, so she must have been in the shower. Relieved, I set down the leftover food I'd grabbed and walked around, just picking up a little bit.

Lark came out of the bathroom in her towel as I was unloading the dishwasher.

I looked up and we both stared at each other for a few seconds.

"Hey," she said. "You were down there for a while."

"Yeah, just talking to Layne and Joy. Didn't realize how much time had passed," I said.

"Right, yeah," she said, shifting from foot to foot. I swallowed, imagining her dropping the towel and letting me lick all the water from her body before fucking her on the couch until she screamed my name.

"I have cake," I said. "If you wanted any more."

"Oh, thanks. I think I'm good right now," she said, starting to walk toward her room.

"It's in the fridge if you change your mind," I said, and she reached for her doorknob.

"Thanks," she said again. "Well, goodnight."

We didn't usually say goodnight to each other, but what else was there to say?

"Goodnight, Lark," I said as she slammed her door shut.

I HAD to work a few hours on Saturday at the shop for my mom, and when I came back upstairs to the apartment, Lark was laughing with someone I didn't know.

"Hey," I said, closing the door and taking off my boots.

"Hey, this is Mia," Lark said as the woman with curly red hair and a face full of freckles waved at me. It took a few seconds to place her as the awkward teen I had seen in the halls in school.

"Right yeah, you were a few years behind me. Nice to see you," I said, shocked that Clem hadn't run over to yell at me. It wasn't until I saw him sleeping in Lark's lap that I relaxed.

"I think I was a freshman when you were a senior. Feels like a million years ago. Nice to see you again too," Mia said, smiling. She was terribly cute, and I wondered if she had a crush on Lark. Or if Lark had a crush on her.

The idea of either of those made me feel sick.

"We're going to go over to Nick's and have pizza if you wanted to come," Mia said, and I didn't think it was my imagination that Lark shot her a quick glare.

"Oh, I was just going to have leftovers," I said. Mia nudged Lark.

"Pizza is better than leftovers," Lark said. "Come with us."

"Okay," I said immediately before I could even think about it.

"Great!" Mia said. She reminded me a little bit of Joy. Bright and enthusiastic. She hopped up from the couch and skipped to the bathroom.

"You don't have to come with us," Lark said in a low voice.

"Do you not want me to come?" I asked.

"No, I do," she said, and then sighed. "Please, come, Sydney."

Fuck. Those words didn't mean anything dirty, but that didn't stop me from thinking very, very dirty thoughts.

"I just have to grab a different jacket," I said in a strangled voice as I ran to my room. "Be back in a sec."

I closed the door of my room and shut my eyes to try and get a little composure. Normally I always had a bit of a filthy mind, but around Lark? It was every other thought. I had to get a hold of myself. Trying to function while constantly horny was not easy.

I did my best to think of all the unsexy things I could as I went to my closet and grabbed the jacket that I'd come in here to get so I didn't look like a liar.

Lark and Mia were waiting for me when I came out. Mia had a smile on her face as she bounced on her toes.

"Ready?" Lark asked me.

"Yup. Let's go."

SINCE NICK'S was so close, we walked since it was a little ridiculous to drive. It was fucking freezing outside, and I'd forgotten to bring gloves, so I shoved my hands in the pockets of my warmest winter jacket.

Mia kept up a light chatter, asking me questions about myself that I tried to give her friendly answers for. She was nothing but nice, but my focus was on a strangely silent Lark.

I held the door for them, and Lark brushed by me to walk in, refusing to meet my eyes.

Nick greeted us with a warm smile and told us the specials. I ate there so much that I knew immediately what I wanted, but Lark and Mia needed time, so they both took menus and stood to the side as they decided. The warmth of the restaurant had started to thaw my frozen fingers by the time everyone had placed their orders and we went to grab a table.

Mia inhaled deeply. "I love the smell of pizza places."

All three of us looked up as we heard yelling coming from the kitchen, but it was just Nick arguing with his husband, which was all part of the atmosphere at Nick's. I didn't understand Greek, but the tone was always playful banter.

Our garlic knot appetizers arrived first, and I grabbed them from the counter and carefully brought them back to the table.

They were absolutely drenched in garlic butter that I knew was going to get all over my hands, but I didn't care.

"Your mom makes mugs, right?" Mia asked out of the blue, and it took me a second to realize what she was asking me.

"Yeah, she does."

"Has she ever sold them on consignment? I bet Liam would love to support a local business and carry them at the coffee shop," she said, taking care as she selected a garlic knot.

"I'd have to talk to my mom about it, but if Liam's on board, I'd love to sit down and talk with him." It was a great idea, and I was kind of mad I hadn't thought of it myself.

"Great, I'll ask him," she said, giving me a wide smile.

Lark was still quiet, eating her garlic knots methodically.

Mia carried the conversation on her back, while Lark gave one-word answers. At last, our food was ready and I was grateful for the distraction.

I didn't realize how hungry I was and tore into my Greek salad.

"Lark told me she joined your book club and I was wondering if they're accepting new members?" Mia asked as she ate her chicken ranch pizza.

"It's not my book club, but yeah, it's always open to anyone who wants to join. The majority of the books we read are queer, though, just so you know," I said. I braced myself for her to say never mind, she didn't want to join, but her face lit up.

"That's perfect! So I can join anytime?"

I told her to send a message to Joy so she could get all the details. She had plenty of time to read our newest book to catch up.

"Yay, I'm so excited now. I can't believe I didn't know about this sooner," Mia said.

"We'd be happy to have you." Something told me Mia would be a great and energetic addition to book club.

We finished our pizza and walked back to the apartment.

"I'm so sorry to eat and run, but I have to get home," Mia said. She hugged Lark and said she'd see her at work on Monday and gave me a little wave as she walked through the door.

Then she was gone, and the apartment was so quiet, I could hear the pitter patter of Clementine's feet on the floor as he ran over to yell at me about food.

"Did you maybe want to watch a movie?" I asked her tentatively.

Lark finally looked at me. "Sure," she said, but she didn't sound enthused.

What was up with her?

I fed Clementine and then filled the kettle to make tea because it seemed like the right thing to do.

"Want some?" I asked as I filled my mug.

Lark nodded. Okay, I guess she had gone nonverbal with me. That wasn't a good sign.

I fetched her a mug as she went through our tea selection and picked out a calming blend. Hmm.

We carried our mugs to the couch, and I picked up the remote to go through the selections.

"What are you in the mood for?" I asked.

Lark just shrugged, staring off into space.

Clenching my teeth, I set my mug and the remote down.

"What the fuck is up with you?" I could just picture Joy

admonishing me for being so blunt with Lark, but I knew she could take it.

Her eyes went wide.

"Nothing," she said.

I rolled my eyes. "Okay, so you've been almost completely silent for hours because of nothing, sure."

Lark sighed. "Leave me alone."

"Fine," I said. If that was what she wanted, I'd leave her alone.

The only problem was, I didn't want to leave her alone. I wanted to do the opposite of that. I wanted to crawl in her lap and kiss her senseless. I wanted to touch and taste every single inch of her. I wanted to strip her naked and worship her body for hours.

Instead of doing any of those things, I sat on the couch and drank my fucking tea and didn't touch her. I selected a movie at random and put it on. Lark didn't object.

She'd curled up in a corner of the couch, as if she was trying to get as far away from me as she could, while still being on the couch.

Deciding to be kind of an asshole, I stretched my legs out, taking up as much room as possible. My legs rested next to her as I slouched down until I was covering the whole surface, except for the corner she occupied.

She made a huffing sound and glared at me.

"Do you mind?" she asked.

"No, I'm very comfortable," I said, wiggling into the cushions and giving her a smile.

Lark rolled her eyes and turned back to the screen, but I could tell she was uncomfortable.

She tried to shift, but there wasn't really any room for her, and she couldn't move without touching me.

I let out what I hoped sounded like a contented sigh.

"This couch is *so* cozy," I said.

Lark looked at me through narrowed eyes. "I know you're trying to piss me off."

"Is it working?" I asked. I'd take pissed off over nothing. I'd take pissed off over indifference.

Lark looked up at the ceiling. "What do you want from me, Sydney?"

She never called me Syd. Always my full name.

"I don't want anything from you," I said.

She scoffed and glanced back at me. "You're trying to annoy me so I'll talk to you. Something a toddler does to get their parent's attention."

"Yes, but it's working, so maybe the toddlers have the right idea."

I nudged her with my foot. I knew I was being a little bit of an asshole, but that wasn't unusual for me. I kept pushing her and waiting to see how she'd react.

"Stop it," she said, shoving at my feet until they fell off the couch. Unfortunately, she shoved so hard that the rest of my body followed, and I ended up in a heap on the floor. Thankfully, Joy had fallen in love with a very plush rug and I'd gotten to keep it when she moved out, so I didn't have any major injuries.

"Shit," I said, looking up at Lark from the floor. She had a smirk on her face as she unfurled her body and stretched out like I'd been doing.

"Ahhh," she said. "This couch *is* comfortable."

I leaned on the edge of the couch and looked up at her. "Now who's being annoying?"

"I'm not being annoying, I'm retaliating," she said. I sat up a little more and gently stroked her leg. She still had her jeans on so I couldn't feel her skin, but it was better than nothing.

"Stop it," Lark said softly.

"Do you really want me to stop?" I asked.

After a few moments, she slowly shook her head back and forth.

"That's what I thought," I said, rising up on my knees and then crawling over to her upper half.

Her eyes didn't leave my face as I leaned in and brought my face within an inch of hers and paused. Lark didn't move back.

"What are you doing?" she whispered.

"Waiting for you to kiss me," I said. "I'm ready. Are you?"

"You're awfully sure of yourself, aren't you?" Lark said.

"I'm sure when I'm right. And I know you want to kiss me," I said.

Lark snorted softly, her breath washing over my face.

"No, I don't want to kiss you," she said, but her voice trembled a little. My knees hurt a little from kneeling, but I'd deal with it if it got me what I wanted.

"Liar," I said, and purposefully licked my lips slowly. Her pupils dilated and her eyes flicked down to watch me.

"Shut the fuck up," she said and then her mouth crashed into mine. Our noses bumped, and my eyes started to water, but I couldn't stop kissing her. For someone who said she didn't want to kiss me, she was absolutely kissing me.

The kiss was almost brutal in its intensity, as if she was almost mad at me for the kiss. I could work with that.

I put my hand on the side of her face, stroking down to her neck where her pulse fluttered like the beat of hummingbird wings.

Fuck, I needed this. I needed Lark's kisses in my life. I needed all of her in my life. Just existing in the same space with her wasn't enough.

She made a little frustrated sound, and I could tell that the angle wasn't right, so I straddled her hips and looked down at her.

"Is this better?" I asked.

"Yeah," she said before reaching for my shirt to pull me back down to her mouth.

This time her mouth was softer, more sensual. As if she was savoring me. I gave her everything she wanted, and a little bit more. She deserved more. She deserved the best kiss I could give her.

Lark's tongue teased mine and I let her explore and do as she wished before I did the same. I savored every single lick and taste and drank her in like she was a glass of the world's best wine.

It took a lot of willpower not to just go right for her clothes to get her naked as quickly as possible, but I'd said this was going to be a kiss, and unless she pushed for more, it was going to stay a kiss, even though my body was on top of hers, and my hips had started a rhythmic thrust into hers. I couldn't help it. Just a little more friction and I would absolutely come. I'd been vibrating on the edge of coming pretty much since she moved in.

"Wait," she said, pulling back and inhaling deeply. I sat up, panting and shaking with need. If she stopped this right now, I needed to go to my room immediately and get off.

"What is it?" I asked, stroking one of her curls. She was so fucking beautiful it was like staring into the sun.

"What are we doing?" she asked.

"Kissing," I said.

"I know that," she snapped. "But what are we *doing*?"

"Whatever we want. We're both consenting adults," I said. I couldn't stop touching her hair. It was so soft, and the spring of her waves made me happy.

"But we're roommates. We shouldn't…" she trailed off as I raked my fingernails over her scalp.

"What shouldn't we do?" I asked.

"This," she said. "Things could get messy. Really messy."

"Mmm, I like messy. Big fan," I said.

"Emotionally messy, Sydney. I don't think you're into that," she said.

I mean, she had me there. Getting my emotions tangled together with my hookups wasn't my thing. It was one of the reasons why I only liked to be with someone once and then send them on their way. Sexual ships passing in the night before moving on to new adventures. I wasn't made for forever. I was made for tonight.

"That's what I thought," Lark said, pushing at me to get off her. Reluctantly, I got to my feet and Lark sat up, running a shaking hand through her hair.

"This is a bad idea for a million and one reasons, Sydney. I think we should cool it off before one of us gets hurt."

"I wouldn't get hurt," I said automatically.

She looked at me and sighed. "But I might, and I don't want that, Sydney. It's best if we just leave things here and move on."

Well, fuck fucking fuck. This night had not gone how I'd planned. The girl I'd been kissing just a few minutes ago was telling me we could never do it again.

I wanted to argue with her. I wanted to throw a tantrum on the floor and scream and beg her and completely embarrass myself if it would make her change her mind.

"That's how you feel?" I asked.

"That's how I feel," she said, nodding. "I think we should go to our rooms for the rest of the night and cool off."

I didn't feel like I was ever going to cool off after that kiss. I was completely on fire. Every single one of my cells burned for her. But I wasn't going to beg. I wasn't going to tell her all the reasons we could hook up and then move on with our lives. She had made up her mind, and it would be wrong of me to try and change it.

So I nodded, turned, and walked to my bedroom. I shut the door without looking back at her. I only opened it when

Clementine meowed on the other side. I glanced toward the couch, but Lark had already gone to her room.

THE NEXT WEEK was one of the most miserable weeks I'd had in my life. Lark barely spoke to me, stayed in her room, or went and hung out at Mia's house. It was ridiculous to say, but I missed her. I missed just talking to her. I wanted to know how her week had gone, if she'd had any funny customers, what she wanted to have for dinner, everything.

Even my mom noticed something was off.

"You've been a total grump this week, Sydney," she said on Thursday. "Is something wrong?"

"Nothing a million dollars couldn't fix," I said, trying to smile.

"Wouldn't that be nice?" she said. "If only we could go viral and get on one of those favorite things list from that talk show host."

"I don't think that's how it works," I said. Mom shrugged.

"Maybe someone famous will vacation here and come into the shop," Mom said.

"Maybe," I said. It wasn't as good as a celebrity, but I had made a consignment deal with Liam for some of our mugs, which was nice. He was a genuinely good guy, and it had been really nice to catch up with him. He'd even asked me about having his girlfriend, Gwen, join book club. She worked as a nurse, but loved to read in her spare time, but was newer to the romance genre. We had a long talk about books, and I came home late, but at least I hadn't had to be in the apartment with Lark ignoring me.

Mom drifted away and that was about as much parental attention as I needed from her.

Joy called me that night and had insisted that we needed to

hang out that weekend and I had the feeling that she and Layne had had at least one talk about me.

"We are going away this weekend and you have no say in it," Joy said. "This is an emergency friend trip."

We hadn't done one of those since we went away for a week, and that was before Layne and Honor had gotten together.

"Where are we going?" I asked as I put the phone on speaker and pulled my rolling suitcase out of my closet.

"To a cabin in the woods, so pack layers."

I made a face. That didn't sound like my cup of tea at all. I'd much rather head to a hotel in a city with some sort of nightlife or activities within walking distance.

"Stop making that face, Syd," Joy said.

"How did you know I was making a face?" I asked.

"Because I know you, Sydney Sparks. Listen, we're not going to force you to use an outhouse or something. We're going to sit inside and drink too much wine and read and gossip." I had to admit, that sounded amazing. Just what I needed.

"Cozy vibes, got it," I said, pulling some sweaters from my closet and tossing them in the suitcase. I added scarves, warm socks, jeans, sweatpants, and a pair of cozy slippers. There. That was the basics. Now I needed more.

I threw in anything I thought I could possibly need, including my favorite vibrator and charger, a screwdriver set, extra sheets, a salt lamp, batteries, extra toilet paper, an air freshener, and a few other things. I didn't stop until I was certain I had anything I could possibly want. Of course, that also meant I had to get out my second larger suitcase to fit everything. It was foolishness to think I could fit everything in my smaller one. I'd never been able to do that, not even for a weekend.

I set both suitcases near the door and sat on my bed. There

was nothing else to do tonight to prep for the trip except toss in my toothbrush in the morning after I used it, so I reached for the top book on my cozy mystery stack and cracked the spine. Since I went through them pretty fast, I either bought them used, or I'd buy new and donate them to the library or the little used section at Mainely Books if I decided not to keep them.

Even though I'd been doing my best to leave Lark alone, I could still hear almost every move she made in the apartment. I heard when she talked to Clementine and when she went into the living room. Lark always talked softly to him and sometimes I heard him meow back to her, as if they were having a conversation. I did the same thing with him, and it made me feel some kind of way when Lark did it too. She also sometimes sung in the shower and I'd press my ear up against the wall just to listen.

I'd always enjoyed my alone time, but now I was having far too much of it, so I was relieved for the weekend trip.

ON FRIDAY AFTERNOON I said goodbye to Mom and went back to the parking lot where Joy was waiting with Layne.

"Are you ready for a friendship adventure?" Joy asked as I got in the backseat after shoving my suitcases in the back.

"I don't know about that, but I'm ready to get away," I said through a yawn.

"Tired?" Layne asked, looking back at me with concern.

"Haven't been sleeping well," I said. I didn't tell them the reason I wasn't sleeping well was named Lark Conroy. I just kept waking up and not being able to get back to sleep. It was seriously annoying. I hoped this cabin they'd rented had nice beds.

"I'll take care of the food budget, since you guys split the cost of the cabin," I said. I wanted to contribute more, but I'd already lost that fight with Joy and I didn't think I would have any better luck with Layne.

"It's only about an hour north, and I found a grocery store nearby," Layne said.

"There's a grocery store? It's a miracle," I said. They both pretended that they didn't hear me.

Chapter Eight

"GROCERY STORE" was a little bit generous for the general store and gas station Joy pulled into. We'd driven further and further into the woods and I was starting to have anxiety about being so far away from civilization.

"I hope we can even find enough food in here," I said, dubious about the selection.

"Come on," Layne said, linking her arm with mine and dragging me inside as Joy filled up the car with gas.

Surprisingly, the store was pretty well-stocked, and we filled two baskets with food and drinks for the next two days. Layne did more of the work to plan out the meals, so I let her get whatever she felt like making and handed over my card when we went to the register.

We crammed the bags into the car and drove about fifteen more minutes until Joy turned down an unpaved, one-lane road.

"This is my nightmare," I said under my breath. There was no snow in the forecast, or else I would have really been freaked out. Being snowed in here would be the worst thing I could imagine.

"Oh, it's so cute," Layne said as Joy parked next to a small rustic cabin with a wrap-around porch and a view over a little pond that was currently frozen over.

"I bet we could go skating on that if we'd brought skates," Joy said. "Next time."

"Let's just get through this weekend alive," I said as we all piled out of the car.

~

LESS THAN TWO hours later I had a glass of wine in my hand, there was a fire in the fireplace, Layne was cooking a rich beef stew for dinner, and I was starting to feel like I might be able to take a short vacation from my drama with Lark.

Of course, as soon as I thought her name in my mind I pictured her, and that led to replaying that fucking kiss we'd had on the couch and then that opened the door to numerous other fantasies of what could have happened if she hadn't stopped me.

Joy sat down on the green plaid couch with me and curled her feet up.

"How's it going?" She'd been in the kitchen helping Layne chop potatoes, but Layne had since kicked her out to finish. I would have shoved my way in, but Layne was happily humming away, so we let her do her thing.

"It's going just fine," I said, sipping my wine and savoring it. Sure, it was probably cheap, but it tasted good to me.

Joy leaned closer to me. "Got anything you want to talk about?"

"Not right now," I said, still staring into the fire.

"If you do, let me know. We've got all weekend."

Layne joined us, since the stew needed to cook on the stove for a little while.

"Okay, who's first pick for comfort movies?" Layne asked.

"Me," I said, even though it was supposed to be Joy. The entire theme of this weekend was to chill out and do nothing, so we'd agreed to watch all our individual comfort movies.

Layne grabbed the remote and turned on the TV and scrolled through.

"Okay, what are we watching?" she asked.

"*Gone Girl*," I said, and they both stared at me. "What? It's one of my comfort movies. You're not supposed to judge my choice, we made a pact."

There were other, softer movies I could have chosen, but that was my pick right now.

"Okay," Layne said with a sigh. "Syd's first choice is *Gone Girl*."

"Let's go," I said as Layne started the movie.

"OKAY, I have to admit that was a good choice," Joy said when the credits started to roll.

"See? I know what I'm doing," I said. Throughout the movie, we'd all sort of melted together into a pile on the couch under two blankets.

"Perfect timing because the stew should be ready," Layne said, stretching her arms and getting up. Good timing because I was absolutely starving.

We all filled our bowls with stew topped with biscuits and sat together at the little dining table.

"To a relaxing and renewing weekend," Layne said, raising her glass.

"Amen," Joy said, and we clinked our glasses together and dug into the stew that was so thick and rich, I almost moaned.

All of us had second bowls before heading back to the couch for Joy's comfort movie, which was *The Princess Bride*. Of course.

Before watching Layne's movie, *The Little Mermaid*, we made tea and popcorn, and Layne arranged us a snack plate with cheese and crackers and some fruit.

My eyes started closing not even halfway through the movie and when it ended, we all agreed we were ready for bed. The cabin had three bedrooms, which was perfect, so I headed upstairs to one of the small rooms with a bathroom that led to another bedroom where Joy stayed. Layne got the master on the first floor again. She always seemed to draw the biggest room when we went away, and I didn't know if she was using dark magic, or if she just had good luck.

THE NEXT TIME I opened my eyes, it was morning and I could hear and smell the sounds of cooking downstairs. I was glad for the wine, because it had led me to completely pass out and sleep dreamlessly for the first time in a while.

I'd needed this weekend more than I could say.

When I stumbled down the stairs with a yawn, I was greeted by Joy at the stove and Layne at the counter doing prep.

"Good morning, love. We were wondering if you were going to stay in bed. We would have kept a plate warm for you," Layne said. I slid into one of the chairs at the dining table next to the kitchen.

"No, I'm up," I said through another yawn.

"You can go back to bed, if you want. This weekend is all about recharging, and if your body needs sleep, then your body needs sleep," Layne said.

"I'm good. I think I can handle a day of reading and watching movies and having snacks," I said.

"There's a little hiking trail behind the cabin that we might take a short walk on," Layne said. "Totally optional."

I sighed, because a walk was probably a good idea. It would be beautiful outside, and I needed to move my body. I walked around the pottery shop a lot during the week, but I needed to add more movement to my life. I had no qualms about doing a yoga practice in the living room or a quick cardio workout when I'd lived with Joy, but after Lark had moved in, I'd stopped doing anything like that and it was starting to affect me.

"Sounds like a plan. After breakfast?"

Joy dished out French toast slathered in Nutella, with spicy potatoes. I'd brought my emergency hot sauces to add an extra kick. My coffee was mixed with Layne's hot chocolate to make a creamy thick mocha and I wanted to drink five hundred cups of it.

No one said anything about Lark directly until we had put on our boots and ventured outside and onto the trail marked with a handmade wooden sign. Thankfully, there were spray-painted markers to help keep us from getting lost, and Layne kept track of where we were via the GPS on her phone.

"So," Joy said as we tromped along, crunching the frost-covered leaves under our feet, "are you going to talk about the Lark situation or not?"

I looked up into the trees and sighed.

"We kissed," I said. They still didn't know we'd kissed several times, and we'd also had sex. If I had my way, they never would.

"And?" Joy prompted.

"And then she said we shouldn't ever do it again and then basically ignored me last week. She thinks that if we were to hook up, that it would get too messy being roommates and that we should just cut our losses now."

I purposefully stepped on a branch to hear a satisfying crack as it broke under my foot.

"And you obviously don't agree with that," Layne said, reading my tone.

"Obviously not," I said. "I know why she's resistant. I do. But I really think we can just do this, get over it, and be fine after. I've done it before."

Layne and Joy shared a look. "Have you, though?" Layne asked gently. "You don't usually hook up with people you're going to talk to after, let alone share a living space with."

I let out a frustrated sound. "It's fine. If she doesn't want to do it, then there's nothing I can do about that. I just need to wait for this fire to burn itself out."

Layne and Joy shared another look, and I was beginning to get annoyed by it.

"Maybe my hookup hiatus was a bad idea," I said. Not having sex is what had gotten me here, so the solution might be going back to having sex. I'd check out my dating sites later. Sure, the last time I'd been on them had been a disaster, but I could try again. I just needed to vet my potential partners better.

It was time for me to get back in the game with someone new.

AFTER OUR WALK, we defrosted in the cabin and Joy made lunch of grilled ham and cheese sandwiches with spinach, and leftover stew. I didn't know if it was the walk, but I was absolutely ravenous.

Post lunch, we all found a cozy spot and pulled out the books we'd brought. I was determined to get through at least three cozy mysteries during this trip, and I'd also brought backup books just in case my mood changed, or I finished early. Another reason I wanted to get over this thing with Lark was to just get back to my regular life. She'd affected my eating and sleeping and reading and I hated it.

"Afternoon snack?" Layne asked in a cheerful voice as I finished the last few pages of the first cozy mystery.

"Yes, please," I said as she handed me a plate. I'd pulled one of the overstuffed green plaid chairs that matched the couch to the window that had a perfect view of the birdfeeder. Joy had kept the fire going and the crackling had lulled me into a meditative reading space.

I munched on the cracker plate as I finished the book and set it aside before reaching for the next one.

My phone went off before I could open the cover and I looked down to find a message from Lark.

I opened it up and was instantly alarmed.

Clementine just puked on the floor, is that normal? She sent.

I was going to need more information, so I called her.

"Hey," I said. "Is he acting sick?"

"No, he's just doing his thing. He puked and then ran under your bed for a few minutes, but now he's at the window yelling at the birds like normal." Her voice was panicked, as if she was on the edge of tears. "I cleaned it up, but I don't know what to do. Should I take him to the vet?"

"I'm sorry to ask you this, but can you describe the consistency of the puke?" I asked.

For people who weren't used to cats, them getting sick could be really alarming the first time, but sometimes, kitties just ate their food too fast, which I was pretty sure was the case with Clem. I couldn't blame him, I got excited about food too.

Lark calmed down a little, and I told her to call me back with video so I could see Clementine for myself. She did and he was at the window, trying to attack the birds and didn't seem to be suffering any ill effects from getting sick, so I told her to monitor him for the rest of the day, give him fresh food and water, and update me if he stopped eating or drinking, or started acting sick.

"Okay, okay, I will," she said, coming back on the video. Her forehead was pinched with worry, and all I wanted to do was reach through the screen and smooth it away with my fingers before kissing her until she felt better.

It wasn't going to happen, and she'd said she didn't want anything like that, so I just thanked her for taking care of Clementine and told her I had faith in her.

"Okay," she said, sitting on the couch. "I'll keep my eye on him and update you if anything changes."

"Sounds good. I'll talk to you later," I said.

"Bye," she said softly before ending the call.

I sat back in my chair and let out a breath.

"Everything okay?" a voice asked, and I jumped as I realized both Layne and Joy had been eavesdropping on my drama.

"Clementine got sick and Lark panicked. I think he's fine, but I wanted to check in and make sure," I said, setting my phone down on the windowsill.

"Oh, poor Clem. Tell Lark to give him a kiss for me," Joy said. "I'm going to convince Ezra to get a cat because I miss having one around."

"Honor has said no cats, but I think I might be able to sell her on a dog," Layne said. "Lark sounded really stressed out."

"I know," I said, chewing my lip. "I hope she's not too worried. It's not her fault my cat is an idiot. He's orange, it's in his nature."

"I'm sure it will be fine," Joy said, rubbing my shoulder as if I was the one who needed comforting.

"Yeah, I know," I said, looking outside as a bright red cardinal landed on the birdfeeder. "I just wish she wasn't so stressed."

I looked back over at Layne, who was typing on her phone.

"I'm going to have Honor drop by."

"She doesn't have to do that," I said. It wasn't as if Honor knew anything about cats.

"Too late, she's on her way," Layne said.

I huffed. I wasn't mad that Honor was going to check on Lark. I was upset I couldn't be the one to do it.

"I need more chocolate," I said.

"You know," Joy said with a sly smile. "We did buy some Kahlua to add to our hot chocolate."

"I'll handle this one," I said. That way I could pour generously.

"Don't forget the whipped cream!" Layne said as I made my way to the kitchen.

THE THREE OF us got a tiny bit wasted on the adult hot cocoa drinks, so we all ended up heading to our rooms for naps before dinner. When I woke up, I found Layne in my room with a glass of water.

"Please hydrate," she said.

I gulped the water down and got up, still feeling a little bit buzzed from the hot cocoa as I headed downstairs with Layne. Joy was already in the kitchen by the stove.

"That smells good, what are we having?" I asked.

"Ravioli lasagna," she said.

"Sounds perfect," I said, stretching my arms over my head and hearing my spine crack a little bit.

My phone had a new message and I looked at it to find a picture of Lark sitting on the couch with a sleeping Clementine.

Just wanted to check in. He's been good the rest of the day and has eaten again and had some water she sent.

That was a relief. I hadn't been that concerned, but you never knew with cats. Animals had a habit of throwing a wrench in your plans when you least expected it.

Neither Joy or Layne asked me again about Lark, although they did ask for updates on Clementine. We all settled in for more comfort movies, and thanks to the naps, we were able to stay up late having more hot cocoa and making each other laugh too much.

Before we packed up and went back on Sunday afternoon, we took another walk. I'd gotten a message that morning while I was still asleep from Lark with a Clementine update that all was well. I told her that we'd be back in the afternoon and I'd take over cat duties from her.

It wasn't that bad, but can you ask him not to scare me like that next time? She sent.

I'll see what I can do, but no promises I responded.

"HAVE YOU BEEN A TROUBLEMAKER?" I asked Clementine immediately when I got back, and he greeted me at the door.

He meowed loudly and wound himself around my legs as if he hadn't seen me in a year.

"You scared poor Lark, you dumbass," I said with an affectionate voice.

"He did," Lark said, getting up from the couch. My breath caught in my chest as she walked over to me. It seemed the cat crisis had thawed some of the coldness she'd put between us.

"How was your trip?" she asked, leaning against the kitchen counter.

"Good," I said. "We did a lot of reading and watching movies and eating and drinking. Couldn't ask for anything better with your two best friends."

Lark nodded and worried at her bottom lip.

"I'm sorry," she said.

"About what?" I asked, untying my boots and shucking them off.

"About treating you like you're not here this week," she said. "I think I was trying to give you space and took it a little too far."

"I was trying to give you space too," I said. "That's what you asked for."

Was she changing her mind? I tried not to get my hopes up at the prospect.

"I did, and that's still what I think is right, but it didn't mean that I needed to stop talking to you or acting like you weren't in the same room. I'm sorry for that. I hope we can go back to being roommates again."

I mean, we'd never really been roommates to begin with. We'd slept together even before we'd moved in, which was always going to be a strange dynamic.

I wanted to argue with her. I wanted to point out how wrong she was. I wanted to set out all my reasons why we could absolutely have a physical relationship and be fine as roommates.

But I didn't say anything like that.

"Yeah, we can," I said. The words *I missed you* stuck in my throat. My weekend had been a good and welcome respite from my life, but still. I had missed her, even though we'd been in touch.

"Good," she said.

There was a heavy pause between us.

"I should unpack," I said. I had laundry to do as well.

"Right, of course. I'll let you get to that." She pushed off the counter and went back to the couch.

Clementine followed her.

"Traitor," I whispered after him.

Chapter Nine

"THINGS ARE BETTER," I told Joy at our lunch the next day. "I mean, she talks to me now, which is an improvement. I think maybe when she pulled back, that that made me want her more, so now that I'm getting regular contact with her, the crush should go away."

I hated even calling what I felt for Lark a "crush." It felt like something a teenager would have. Frivolous and unserious.

"Sounds like a plan," Joy said and then pressed her lips together as if she was stopping herself from saying anything more.

"What?" I asked. "Come on, say it."

"No, nothing. I'm keeping my opinions to myself."

I raised my eyebrows. "Oh really? When have you ever done that before?"

She smacked me lightly on the arm.

"Hey. I'm doing my best. I'm trying to focus on myself and less on other people now," she said.

"Is that from Ezra's influence?" I asked. Being with Ezra had had other impacts on Joy, all positive.

"Sort of. She also helped me set some better boundaries

with my family. My mom isn't happy, but she's dealing with it, and I feel better when I go to visit," she said.

That was a relief. Joy and her family had a complicated relationship, especially between Joy and her mom.

"I'm happy for you, that's great, Joy." She beamed.

"Thanks."

We finished our lunches and hugged before heading back to our jobs.

"Good luck with Lark," Joy said before she pushed the door of the bookshop open. I gave her the finger.

I CAME HOME from work on Wednesday evening to find Lark on the couch. She was home early from work.

"Hey," I called, and she answered me with a cracked voice.

I set my shit down and went to see what was up. Lark looked awful. Her eyes were red and puffy, her nose was clearly running, and even her hair was limp and flat.

"Oh no, are you okay?" I asked. Clementine was making biscuits by her feet with the blanket.

"I felt shitty yesterday, but then it really hit me today. Liam sent me home after lunch," she said, and then had a coughing fit. "I'm sorry if you get sick."

"No, that's fine. It's kind of what happens when you live with people. Layne used to be sick all the time when the twins were little. Kids are germ factories."

Lark nodded and sniffed. She reached for the tissue box she'd set on the table, but it was empty. Lark frowned and set it down with a sigh. I dashed to my room and came back with my personal box.

"What do you need?" I asked.

"Oh, I'm fine," she said as she blew her nose.

"Have you taken anything?" I asked.

She shook her head and closed her eyes.

"Maybe you could make me some tea?" she asked.

I'd do better than that.

First, I went to take inventory of the meds in the bathroom. I brought her some cold medicine, along with a ginger ale to wash it down before I filled the kettle for tea.

Fortunately, there was a can of chicken noodle soup in the cupboard for just such an emergency, so I got it out to make.

"Have you eaten anything today?" I called to her.

"Um, I had a bagel this morning?" she said, but she didn't sound that sure.

"I'm making you some soup," I said.

Along with her lemon ginger tea, I added some honey and an extra squirt of fresh lemon juice to her cup.

"Try that," I said, giving it to her.

Lark protested as I started to clean up the tissues, but I ignored her.

"Drink your tea," I said, pointing at her.

She looked like she wanted to argue, but she sipped anyway. I gave her the bowl of soup with some oyster crackers once she finished the tea.

I found her some cough drops and then set up the humidifier next to her to help loosen everything up in her chest.

"Sydney, this is too much," Lark said.

"Shut up and eat your soup," I said.

"You know, you'd make a terrible nurse. Your bedside manner is shit," she said.

"Good think I'm not a nurse, then," I said, standing over her to supervise her with the soup. Lark added a few crackers and ate her soup dutifully.

"There you go. Now close your eyes," I said, taking the bowl from her.

"I'm not tired," she said and then yawned.

"Nice try. Close your eyes," I said.

She glared at me briefly before doing as I asked.

Lark was asleep within five minutes.

"That's what I thought," I said softly.

IN ADDITION to throwing something together for myself for dinner and running over to the grocery store for more supplies (including soup), I washed Lark's sheets and changed her bed, threw her pillows in the dryer to fluff, and cleaned the bathroom. There wasn't really a way for me to avoid getting sick, but I still disinfected anything I could anyway.

Lark slept until after I finished dinner and started the dishwasher.

I dosed her with more tea and made her eat some toast and scrambled eggs. I took her temperature and was relieved that it was only a little bit elevated.

"How do you feel?" I asked her, putting my hand on her forehead like my mom used to do. I had no idea what this meant, but she did feel warm.

"Tired," she said.

"I pulled out some clothes for you, so why don't you go change and get into bed. I made it up with fresh sheets and blankets."

"You didn't have to do that," she said. "You're doing too much. I can take care of myself."

"Joy and I always took care of each other when we were sick," I said, maybe a little too harshly.

"I need to pee," she said. "And I feel gross."

"If you're up for a shower, I can put a chair in there for you to sit on so you can relax," I said.

Lark looked like she wanted to argue with me, but she just closed her eyes and swallowed. "Thank you."

I put the chair in and then helped her get up and head to the bathroom.

"I've got it from here," she said, but I put out a fresh towel for her, and brought the pajamas in so she could put them on right away.

"Just toss me your clothes when you're done. I'm going to put the couch blanket in the wash," I said as I closed the bathroom door and let her have some privacy.

I cleaned up and did some more laundry and listened at the bathroom to make sure Lark was okay in there and didn't need any help.

She came out with her hair dripping but wearing her pajamas.

"Let me get your hair," I said, getting another towel from the linen closet and following her to her bedroom.

Lark sat on her bed as I towel-dried her hair and then worked her curl cream through the ends before getting out the tangles with a wide-toothed comb.

"Time for bed," I said, setting another dose of meds and a bottle of water next to her. "Message me if you need anything. I can come up and check on you tomorrow while I'm at work." One of the many benefits of living so close to your work.

Lark settled back on her pillows and sighed.

"Thank you for taking care of me," she said, her voice sleepy.

"It's what roommates do," I said before shutting off her light, turning on the humidifier, and leaving the room.

THAT NIGHT I kept waking up and wanting to go check on Lark. I knew she just had a cold and she wasn't dying of influenza or something, but I couldn't stop wanting to go into the room and take her temperature or force more tea down her throat.

She wasn't normally a snorer, but she was pretty loud that night due to the congestion, but at least she was sleeping.

The next morning I felt like shit, but I told myself it was just due to taking care of her.

"Good morning," I said as I softly knocked on her door and poked my head in. She was awake, but bleary eyed.

"How am I still so tired after sleeping so much," she said, her voice stuffy and nasal.

I bustled in, refilling the humidifier, taking her temperature again, tossing the trash, and bringing her fresh water and more medicine.

"Do you feel any better?" I asked.

"I can't tell," she said. "My whole body hurts, though."

I wished I could take the day off and take care of her. If I didn't have to open the shop, I'd draw her a bath with a really nice bath bomb and then put her back in bed again.

"I made you some toast and a little mug of soup," I said. "Can you get that down before I go? I'll be back to make you lunch."

Lark sat up and ate everything I asked her before getting out of bed to take care of herself in the bathroom.

She had a TV on her dresser, a laptop, and plenty of books, as well as her phone, so I knew she wasn't going to be bored. I was going to leave her door open so Clementine could be a kitty nurse. He'd tried to get in her room every time I had checked on her last night.

Lark came back and coughed a few times before getting into bed again. Clementine was all too happy to jump up and go over to sniff her, recoiling a little bit.

"Listen, sir, she took care of you this weekend, so she doesn't need any judgment from you. Be a good nurse and look after her today," I said, petting his head. Clem meowed like he understood.

"I'm going to leave the door open so he can come and go," I told her. She looked pale and listless.

"I'll see you at lunch, okay?" I said.

"Okay," she said as if her throat hurt.

"Take care of yourself, Lark," I said.

"Mmm," she said before going back to sleep.

MY PHYSICAL BODY might have been down at the pottery shop, but my brain was upstairs with Lark. I tried not to message her phone too much since I knew she was sleeping, so I just told Mom what was going on and that I'd need to run upstairs when it was slow so I could check on her.

"I'm sure she's fine," Mom said. "If she's really that sick with you checking on her so much, she should go to the doctor."

"She's not that sick," I said. "I did the same thing when Joy was sick."

Mom gave me a look. Why was she being so perceptive today? I didn't like it.

I also sent Layne a message that Lark was sick and that she should tell Honor not to worry and that I had it taken care of.

Liam told me she'd gone home early yesterday, poor thing. Let me know if you need anything. I can whip you up some soup today. I've got the time she sent.

That would probably be better for Lark than the stuff in a can.

Could you? That would be amazing I responded.

No problem at all. I can check on her too she sent.

You are the best, Layne I replied.

My girlfriend would agree with you she responded.

She still hadn't proposed to Honor, but she was getting closer to figuring out her plans. I still thought simple would be better, but Layne was determined to make it big.

Hurry up and make her your fiancée I sent.

Working on it she responded.

∿

LAYNE DROPPED the soup off and sent me a message that Lark was sleeping and looked like she was doing fine.

She was still asleep when I took my lunch break, but I heated up some soup anyway and woke her up to eat it. I sucked down my own bowl while standing at the kitchen counter before heading back downstairs.

Honor messaged me to let me know if we needed anything just to ask.

I'll let you know if her temperature spikes, or she gets worse, I promise I sent.

Lark was awake and sitting up when I came up after closing the pottery shop. Clementine was still on her bed and jumped down to greet me.

"Hey, you look better," I said, and I wasn't lying. Her color was definitely better.

"Thanks," she said. "I feel like I've slept enough for a year."

"Can I get you anything?" I asked.

"No, I'm good," she said. "I was thinking I might like a change of scenery, so I was going to move to the couch."

"Sure, go for it," I said. "I'm just going to put something else on and make some dinner. Do you want more soup?"

"Yes, please. With crackers." Her having an appetite was another positive sign, and her temperature had gone down a tiny bit when I checked it as she lounged on the couch.

Figuring the soup was better than anything I could make, I heated up enough for two servings and grabbed the bag of crackers, along with two cans of ginger ale.

Lark chuckled at something on the TV.

"What are you watching?" I asked as I set the soup and sodas down on the coffee table.

"The gay lady baseball show. Have you seen it?" she asked as I passed her bowl over, being careful not to dump it on her.

"No, but I know Layne loves it," I said.

"You can start it over," she said. "I've only made it to the second episode."

I sat down and started the show over, and she folded her legs up to give me room. Without saying anything, I grabbed her feet and pulled her legs into my lap. Her feet were covered in fuzzy socks, but her legs were bare and warm and so incredibly soft.

I waited for her to protest, but she didn't. She just wiggled her toes a little and settled in as the show started. I picked up my bowl of soup and ate it as normally as I could, given that I had her gorgeous legs in my lap. At least they were under a blanket, so I couldn't see how luscious they were. I could just feel them and feel every movement she made.

Lark had great everything, but her legs were especially perfect. She also had the daintiest feet I'd ever seen on a grown woman. Made me want to paint her cute little toenails for her even though the smell of polish gave me a headache.

The show was adorable and funny, but the best part was hearing Lark's laugh. It was such a relief that she was starting to feel better. Her nose still ran, and she had a coughing fit every now and then, but her eyes were bright and her fever was down.

"Layne makes a mean chicken noodle soup," she said as I took her empty bowl from her.

"Layne makes a mean everything. She can make these

daintily decorated cookies and then turn around and make a three-course dinner for forty people without even breaking a sweat. A woman that knows how to cook under pressure."

"Honor needs that. Neither of us are very good at cooking. Our mother thought cooking was something for other people to do, and she didn't like getting her hands dirty, so Honor and I either ate something prepared by a private chef, or we got really good with the microwave. It's really nice of Layne to help me make up for lost time."

Sometimes I hated hearing about Lark's childhood because nearly every story made me so angry.

She wiggled her toes again and I picked up one of her feet and started rubbing it, mostly just to see her reaction. It was something Joy and I would do for each other, so it wasn't as if this was something I'd never done for a roommate before.

Lark's breath caught and then a few seconds later, she let out what I could only describe as a moan that had me instantly turned on. I'd heard that sound before and all I wanted was to hear it again and again and again.

"That feels good," she said, her voice rough. Even though I was horny as hell, she was sick, so there was no chance of this going any further than me playing with her feet. If I could give her a little bit of comfort, that was enough. I'd store those moans in my brain and get them out later when I was alone in my room with my vibrator.

Clementine hopped up and curled himself on Lark's chest, purring like a freight train.

"Sweet orange boy," Lark said softly as she petted him. "Yes, you're a sweet boy."

Clem purred louder and I switched to Lark's other foot.

We finished another episode and Lark let out a little sigh.

"Do we have any ice cream?" she asked as Clementine tilted his head so she could scratch his ears.

"Yeah, let me check."

If we didn't have ice cream, I was going to go buy her some.

I lifted her feet so I could get up and checked the freezer and found two small containers.

"Do you want mint chocolate chip or brownie batter?" I called.

"Brownie batter!" she said, and then started coughing. I filled the kettle again to make her some more tea with lots of honey, and I added some ground ginger and lemon juice for an extra kick.

"Thank you," she said, reaching for the ice cream. I pushed the cup of tea into her hand.

"Drink that first."

She sighed. "Yes, ma'am."

In normal circumstances, being called "ma'am" made me want to scream, but Lark calling me that? Hot. Super hot.

Lark drank her tea and then grabbed the ice cream and dug in. I went back to rubbing her feet, but my hands had snuck a little bit higher to her ankles and then to her calves.

I waited for her to protest, but she didn't. Lark savored her ice cream as I let my fingers wander up and down her leg, not even massaging, just enjoying touching her. I'd always been a super tactile person, and my little hookup hiatus had left me deprived of touch and I hadn't known how much I needed it. Yet another reason I needed to get off hiatus and start having sex again, if not for the orgasms, then definitely for the closeness.

I'd sort of zoned out and the next time I looked over at Lark, she was fast asleep with the empty ice cream container still clutched in her hand.

CHELSEA M. CAMERON

LARK CONTINUED TO IMPROVE, and by the weekend, she was back to her regular self. Somehow, I'd managed to avoid getting sick, but I knew that something would get me eventually.

Since she'd spent so much time at home in bed or on the couch, she decided to go out after work on Friday with Mia and some other people, so I went to Layne's for dinner with Joy, Ezra, and Honor.

Layne seemed a little weird when she let me in, practically vibrating as if she wanted to tell me something.

"Whoa, what's going on?" I asked as she pulled me inside.

"We have to wait until everyone gets here," she said as Honor came out of the bathroom.

My eyes went immediately to the sparkly ring on the fourth finger of her left hand.

"Oh my god!" I yelled, rushing over and grabbing her hand. She smiled and Layne joined us, giving Honor a kiss.

"Congratulations, it's gorgeous," I said. The ring had an oval diamond in the center, surrounded by more small diamonds and set in gold, almost like flower petals. It had a lovely vintage vibe that was so Honor.

"It's a replica of one from the '20s, but made with lab diamonds," Layne said.

"It's absolutely stunning," I said, turning Honor's hand so the ring glinted in the light. The center stone was massive, so it was definitely going to turn heads.

Joy and Ezra walked in as I admired the ring.

"What are we looking at?" Joy said, coming over and then letting out a shriek and throwing herself at both Honor and Layne as tears streamed down her face. Ezra's reaction was more subdued as she smiled and said, "Congratulations you two."

Joy wiped her eyes on her sleeve. "I'm so happy, tell us everything. How did you do it? Wait! We need champagne."

"I've got us covered," Layne said, going to the fridge and bringing out a bottle of extremely fancy champagne.

Honor got the glasses and Joy was bouncing off the walls and asking a million questions.

Both Layne and Honor were fucking glowing. If we turned off the lights, we'd still see them clearly.

Layne filled our glasses and we went to the living room to hear the whole story.

"A toast," Joy declared. "To Layne and Honor. We're so thrilled for you both. I'm not going to go on and on because I'm saving my most romantic words for the actual wedding. So for now, cheers to love."

"To love," we all said, touching our glasses together and then sipping the bubbly champagne.

Layne and Honor sat together in one of the chairs as if they wished they could meld together into one person. Ezra had her arm around Joy on the couch and I sat next to Joy, trying to give them space.

"I had so many ideas," Layne said. "Helicopters, falcons, the works. And I was stressing the fuck out and one night, I had a nightmare." She smiled at Honor. "And Honor woke me up and asked me what was wrong. I blurted out that I'd had a nightmare about taking her to the top of a mountain to propose and getting attacked by a bear. I had the ring in my nightstand so I didn't lose it and I just yanked it out and said that planning was stressing me out too much so if she could just say yes now, I could go back to sleep."

Joy's mouth dropped open.

"And I said yes," Honor said, smiling at Layne. "It was perfect. I didn't need a mountain. I just needed you to give me the damn ring."

I snorted as they kissed.

"I gave you the damn ring. Now where's mine."

Honor winked at her. "It's coming."

THE CHAMPAGNE WAS DELICIOUS, and dinner was incredible, and the joy that surrounded Layne and Honor was contagious, but there was still something missing.

I wondered what Lark was doing. If she was having fun with Mia. How many drinks she'd had. When she was going to come home. If she would come home.

I left Layne and Honor's earlier than I normally would have, but I told them I was tired. The truth was that I couldn't handle being around two such happy couples. It had definitely gotten to me tonight when I could normally just go with the flow.

Lark wasn't back yet when I walked into the apartment, so I snuggled with Clem on the couch with a new book. I'd gone a little overboard with buying holiday romances and I was still working through them. The disaster lesbian main character was really speaking to me, and the love interest was a butch wedding planner, so what more could you want?

I was almost halfway through the book when I heard some noise outside the door. At first I ignored it, figuring it was just one of the neighbors, but then I heard what sounded like someone trying to put their key in the lock.

Clementine followed me to the door where I looked through the peephole.

"Let me in," an inebriated voice said. From what I could tell, Lark was standing outside with Mia trying to hold her up.

"Hello," Lark said when I opened the door.

"Hey," I said.

Mia's face went a little red. "She had a few at my place, so I brought her back."

"I can take it from here," I told her, reaching for Lark, who stumbled into my arms with a giggle. Oh, she was wasted.

"Thanks," Mia said. "We tried to get her to slow down." She kept trying to explain, but I waved her off.

"It's fine, not a big deal. Thanks for being a good friend."

Mia smiled and then handed me Lark's keys.

"See you later," I said.

"Have a good night." She headed down the stairs and I dragged Lark inside. It was a job to get her to her room. She kept petting my hair and singing.

"Lark, you are a lightweight," I said as I dumped her onto her bed. She giggled and rolled on her side.

"Did you have fun tonight?" I asked as I pulled out some pajamas for her. I didn't think she'd be able to get them on herself without assistance.

Lark squinted at me.

"You're sooooooo hot," she said.

"Thank you," I said. "So are you." Even with snot running out her nose. Even completely wasted like she was now. Lark was always hot.

"Take your clothes off," she said, pointing a wavering finger at me.

"No way. We're not doing anything right now while you're this drunk," I said. "You lay right there and I'm going to get you some water and aspirin and a bucket because I think you're going to need it."

Lark rolled on her back and looked at the ceiling and started singing a nonsense song. I figured that was as good as it was going to get.

Lark didn't fight me as I made her drink a glass of water and a few pills.

"Let's get you into something comfortable, okay?" I said, pulling her until she was sitting up with her legs over the side of the bed.

"Can you get your shirt over your head?" I asked, trying

not to stare at her. Ogling my drunk roommate wasn't something I needed to do.

"I got this," she told me.

"Okay, show me," I said.

Lark pulled her shirt up and then got it stuck on her head.

"I don't got this," she said in a sad voice. "Help."

I stifled a laugh and helped her get the shirt off. I left her bra on and told her to put her arms up so I could get her night shirt on.

Then it was time for her jeans. Thankfully, they were baggy, so they slid right down her legs, and I pulled her sleep shorts on and got her back in bed.

"You're sooooo pretty," Lark slurred at me, her eyes half closed.

"Thank you. You're very pretty too," I said, running my hand through her hair once.

"We should fuck," Lark said.

"Not right now."

"Yesss," she said, frowning. "I want to fuck."

"Tomorrow," I said, knowing she wouldn't have any memory of this conversation. "Close your eyes and sleep now."

"No," she said even as she closed her eyes.

"Your bucket is right next to the bed," I told her as she mumbled something else.

Before I left the room, I leaned over and kissed her on the forehead.

Chapter Ten

THE NEXT THING I heard was someone hurling their guts out in the bathroom. I guess Lark was awake.

I got out of bed and waited until the gagging stopped before I knocked on the door.

"Are you okay?"

"Fuck off," she said.

"Just checking," I said, and headed to the kitchen to make her some hangover food.

Lark took a long time in the bathroom and by the time she came out, I was putting bacon in a pan.

"Well hello there," I said, trying not to be too smug.

"Too loud," she said, one hand holding the side of her head.

"Sorry," I said, lowering my volume. "I'll have breakfast here in a few minutes. Why don't you crash on the couch?"

She just moaned and laid down and didn't move or make a sound until I brought a plate to her with a cup of coffee.

"Bacon, egg, and cheese," I told her as she accepted the plate and grimaced.

"Try a few bites and see how you feel," I said, joining her with my own plate.

"Shh," she said, taking a tiny bite of the sandwich, chewing, and swallowing. She waited a few seconds before taking another tiny bite.

I tried not to watch her too much and busied myself with my own breakfast.

Lark managed to get half the sandwich down and then nursed her coffee. I brought her some more painkillers and another glass of water.

"I'm going to sit here and hope it stays down," she whispered. I just nodded and went to clean up. Quietly.

LARK STARTED LOOKING a bit more chipper as the day wore on. I puttered around doing chores and this and that while she convalesced on the couch.

"I'm never drinking again," she said around dinnertime. I was throwing together a quick chicken sheet-pan meal that Joy had taught me to make.

"Yeah, sure," I said as I shoved the pan in the oven.

"I'm not," she said.

"Okay, Lark," I said.

She glared at me over the edge of the couch. She still looked like she'd had a rough night.

"I'm going to take a shower," she grumbled, getting up.

While she was doing that, I got a message from Joy.

Hey, we need to plan Layne and Honor's engagement party she sent.

They literally just got engaged I responded. I mean, I was all about having a party, but did we have to do it right fucking now?

I know, but I want it to be perfect for them. And I know you'd want to have your input she sent.

I mean, that was true. If she went ahead and planned it without running it by me first, I would be pretty pissed. Plus, she was going to need help.

Okay, hit me I replied.

What came next was a flood of links and even one to a mood board that Joy had already started putting together.

Jesus Joy, you've been busy I sent.

I may have started putting this together when Layne originally told me she was going to propose she responded with a sheepish emoji.

That was so Joy.

I'll look through it and let you know my thoughts. Might take me a few hours I sent with a kissy face emoji.

Lark came out of the shower wrapped in a towel and I kept my eyes on my phone, but that didn't stop me about thinking about all her fresh, clean skin and how much I wanted to get her all dirty again and then take her to the shower again.

My horny feelings toward Lark still hadn't subsided, which meant I just needed to find a new outlet to release them. Falling into bed with someone new was just the remedy.

Since the pickings in Arrowbridge were slim (at least they were for me), I had to expand my search area, and that meant logging back into my online dating profiles and doing some swiping.

At first I just saw a few familiar faces, so I skipped them. I needed new. Someone bright and shiny to hold my attention. Bright eyes and warm skin and enthusiasm.

I found a few candidates and sent some preliminary messages to test the chemistry. The vibes had to be right before I'd hop into bed with someone. Through a lot of trial and error (a LOT), I knew what my instant red flags were, and the kinds of hookups that weren't worth my time.

Lark came out of her room just as I pulled dinner from the oven.

"Is some of that for me?" she asked.

"Yeah, of course," I said. I'd made two portions without even thinking about it.

"Thanks," she said, getting two plates out of the cupboard.

She filled her plate and then we sat together on the couch and watched another episode of the show about teachers. It had quickly become my favorite thing and I was hoping it would get another season.

Joy sent me another message with a link to some decor.

Have you been in touch with Lark about the party? She might also want to be involved I sent.

Yeah, I've been talking with her too. She basically told me whatever I wanted to do was fine, but I'm still keeping her in the loop Joy responded.

"You're smart," I told her, looking up from my phone.

"For any particular reason, or just in general?" she asked.

"For telling Joy to do whatever for the engagement party. She's already sent me about five hundred links and I'm about to tell her to just be in charge."

Lark finished her plate and set it down. "Unless I want to be in charge, I'm happy to step aside and let someone else go for it. When I was growing up, I would just let Honor or my mother do what they wanted because it was just easier not to fight. At least for most things," she said. "My therapist says I should stop doing that."

"No, I see what you're saying. If you don't really care either way, then I understand stepping aside. I'm not good at it. Too much of a control freak," I said, shrugging.

"You're not *that* much of a control freak," Lark said, rolling her eyes.

"I'm controlling myself right now," I said, meeting her

eyes. I should not be going down this road. I should stop talking right now.

"That's not the kind of control we're talking about, Sydney," she said, looking away from me.

I slammed my lips together and didn't say anything else. See? Control.

One of the women I'd messaged on my dating app started chatting with me and she was sweet and funny, and I went ahead and asked her if she wanted to have brunch with me on Sunday. She lived about thirty-five minutes from Arrowbridge, which wasn't too far a commute for sex, so I'd said she could pick a spot that she liked. Honestly, the food wasn't what I was there for. Some people might not think that a mid-day meal could lead to steamy sex, but brunch was an inherently horny meal.

Lark was hanging out with Mia again, so everything had fallen into place for my perfect day. I was a little bit giddy as I got ready in the bathroom and made sure that I looked as fuck-able as possible. Hard to do when you had to cover up with a winter coat and hat and so forth, but I did what I could. I'd left my dark hair down. It was extra shiny and soft from a deep-conditioning treatment I'd done last night. My body was groomed and moisturized and tingling at the thought of being touched and licked and teased.

My skin buzzed with anticipation.

"Mama's getting laid," I announced to Clementine when I stepped out of the bathroom and headed for the door.

Clementine meowed and then went to his window.

"Be a good boy while I'm gone," I said.

Clementine ignored me.

MY ENERGY and excitement started high as I drove toward the restaurant that my date, Nicole, had selected.

But as I got closer, I started feeling…less enthused. I told myself that it was just because I was out of practice. Once I saw her and we started talking and I felt the spark of newness, my libido would take over and do the thinking for me. I couldn't wait.

AT LEAST I found the restaurant, which was at the end of a strip mall of stores.

I let Nicole know I was there, and also sent a message to Layne and Joy as I always did when I had a hookup, letting them know where I was. You could never be too careful.

Nicole told me she was already inside waiting, so I checked myself one more time in the mirror and headed for the restaurant.

I pushed through the door and was hit by a rush of warm air.

"Sydney?" a sweet voice said. I turned and saw a woman who matched the pictures I'd seen online. She was shorter than me and had generous handfuls of curves that I couldn't wait to touch. My mouth started watering just thinking about it.

"Hi, nice to meet you," I said, leaning forward to give her a hug. She hugged me back and I breathed in the scent of her ash-blonde hair. Lovely.

She pulled back from the hug and smiled at me. There was a little gap between her front teeth that was so completely charming, I was patting myself on the back for reaching out to her. I had excellent taste.

A hostess took us to our table, and we made small talk until we ordered. I knew a lot of people hated small talk, but I loved everything about meeting someone new like this. Nicole was exactly what I'd wanted. Bubbly, funny, and completely adorable.

"And that's how I ended up with five cats," she said, finishing a story about coming home and finding a strange cat in her house that ended up having kittens in her closet a few hours later.

"I'd love to see pictures," I said. Nicole smiled and showed me dozens of pictures of the mama cat, Pasta, and her kittens: Penne, Macaroni, Ravioli, and Spaghetti.

"I just have my guy, Clementine," I said, showing her pictures of him.

"Aw, he's just a big orange boy," she said.

"He is," I said.

Our food arrived and everything was going right, but I couldn't ignore a nagging doubt in the back of my head that kept getting louder and louder. *No*, I told it. *I want to be here. I want to have sex with this woman. I want it very much. There is nothing wrong with this desire. Shut the fuck up and let me get laid.*

I kept a smile on my face and listened to Nicole and leaned forward when she asked if I wanted a bite of her pancakes and toasted her with my mimosa.

We finished our plates and I told her I'd take care of the bill. She blushed so prettily and I knew I wanted to kiss her.

"What are you doing for the rest of the afternoon?" I asked.

Nicole's dark brown eyes sparkled. "Absolutely nothing. I live close by, if you wanted to come over for some…tea."

"That sounds perfect," I said, even though the doubt had now developed a voice that screamed *no it's not!*

I ignored it.

WHEN WE GOT OUTSIDE, I told Nicole I'd meet her at her place so I could have my car. She gave me the address and I put it into my phone's GPS. It was only ten minutes away.

The doubt voice yammered away as I drove and then parked in a driveway behind the car I'd seen Nicole get into. Her house was a tiny little cottage that looked a little shabby, but had flowerpots on the small porch, and a sweet fenced-in yard.

"Get out of the car, Sydney," I said to myself as my hands gripped the steering wheel. The little doubt voice had now morphed into a racing heart, a churning stomach, and damp palms.

"What is wrong with you?" I asked myself. "Just go in the house and have sex with the pretty girl. You have done this before a million times." Maybe not that many, but still. It was a lot. So what the hell was wrong with me now? Nicole was incredibly sexy, we'd had a great time, but I could not get out of this car.

"Fuck," I said, slamming my forehead against the steering wheel. The horn beeped and I slammed my head two more times for good measure.

I can't do this.

I couldn't go into this perfectly nice home with this perfectly nice girl and have perfectly nice sex.

I'm so sorry, but I need to head out. Everything was great, but I'm just not ready to be vulnerable with someone right now. I'm so sorry I sent to Nicole and then turned my notifications off as I backed out of her driveway and went back to Arrowbridge.

MY ANNOYANCE at myself grew and grew until it morphed into anger as I made my way back to Arrowbridge. By the time

I pulled into my parking space, I was almost shaking with rage. Now I wanted to drive up to the top of a mountain and scream, but I didn't know if that was going to do it.

I locked my car and stomped up the stairs, unlocking the door with shaking fingers.

Clementine ran over to me, must have sensed that he should leave me alone, and headed for my room. I felt like I was ready to explode.

Lark popped her head up from the couch.

"Hey," she said in a cheerful tone before she saw my face. "Are you okay?"

"No, Lark, I'm not okay," I said. I threw my keys on the floor and kicked off my boots, getting melted snow everywhere.

She got up from the couch and approached me, which only made me madder.

"I swear to god, Lark," I said as she looked at me with those wide blue eyes. Her lips were wet, as if she'd just licked them.

I broke.

Without thinking of the consequences, I walked over to her, put a hand on her chest and pushed her backward into the wall. Our mouths crashed together in a brutal kiss, but she didn't push me away. Didn't ask me what the hell I was doing. No. She kissed me back and wrapped one of her legs around me to bring me closer.

"Fuck," I said into her mouth as we both gasped for air.

"Your room or mine?" she said as I licked and bit my way down her neck, leaving marks on her creamy skin. Good. I wanted to mark her.

My room had all my stuff in it, including my toys and lube, but her door was just a tiny bit closer, and her mattress was newer.

"Yours," I said, and we stumbled our way through her door as I pushed her until she fell back on her bed.

"Take your clothes off," I said as I ripped off my coat and hat and worked on the rest of mine. No time for sexy stripteases. I needed her naked *now*.

Lark pulled off her t-shirt, sweatpants, and underwear in record time and I shimmied out of my jeans and bottoms at the same time.

"Come here," she said, reaching for me and I joined her on the bed. She turned on her side and kissed me and slid her hand down my stomach before she found me wet and trembling. I did the same for her and we fucked each other harshly with our fingers.

I came first, with her bottom lip between my teeth as I slammed my fingers into her as I felt her inner muscles clench around me. Just as I was coming down from my own climax, I felt hers burst through her as she bucked against my hand and let out the sweetest sounds.

In the aftermath, we lay trembling together. My fingers were still inside her and I wiggled them, making her twitch.

Her eyes opened and she leaned back a little bit.

"What the fuck, Sydney?" she said, her chest heaving. Her lips were darker and swollen from me kissing her so hard.

I stroked her with my fingers again, hitting the spot inside that made her hips jerk toward me. Her eyes shuttered closed.

"We should talk," she said in a breathy voice.

"Later," I said, stroking her again and then slipping another finger inside her. "We'll talk later."

I expected her to protest, but she just bit her lip and grabbed my wrist.

"Harder," she said.

～

LARK DIDN'T BRING up talking again until I'd given her at least five orgasms and had gotten five myself. We were both a mess, but neither of us had the energy to move off the bed.

"You know we need to talk," Lark said as I wrapped one of her curls around my damp fingers.

I nodded and met her eyes. "I had brunch with someone today and I was all set to go back to her house and fuck her brains out, but then I was in my car in her driveway and I couldn't. I couldn't fuck her because all I was thinking about was you," I said.

Lark inhaled sharply.

"I got drunk the other night because of you. I couldn't stop thinking about you and all I wanted was to come home and fall into bed with you, so I just…kept drinking and hoping that would help. It didn't."

I traced her face with one finger, lingering on her lips.

"I tried to stop thinking about you. I tried to go fuck someone else and I couldn't get out of my fucking car. So embarrassing. I'm pissed at you, just so you know."

She smiled. "You have an interesting way of being mad at me," she said, pinching one of my nipples.

"Sex and anger can go hand in hand, don't you think?" I asked. "You haven't had a hatefuck before?"

"Uh, no," she said, her cheeks red.

"You should try it. Highly recommend."

She shifted closer to me, putting one of her legs on top of mine. "I'll consider it."

We were quiet for a little while, just touching each other.

"This was a really bad idea," she whispered.

"I *love* bad ideas," I said. "They almost always work out for me. With a few exceptions, but those don't count."

Lark looked into my eyes. "Please don't ruin my life."

I laughed. "If giving you a bunch of orgasms is going to ruin your life, then I'm happy to do that."

She sighed. "Can you be serious for five minutes, please?"

"Fine," I said. "Proceed." I gestured for her to continue.

Lark took a deep breath. "Have you ever been in a relationship, Sydney?"

"What kind of relationship?" I asked. I wasn't being sarcastic.

"A committed one. Have you ever had a girlfriend before?"

"Uhhh, not really," I said. "Not in the way you're talking."

Lark closed her eyes as if that was the answer she'd dreaded.

"Why does that matter? We're just having fun, aren't we?" I asked. "Sex doesn't have to equal girlfriend." At least not for me.

"I've never had a physical only relationship," she said.

"That's okay. I've had lots of experience. I can help you," I said, stroking her stomach.

"I tried not having sex with you and that didn't work," she said.

"Obviously." We'd tried to keep our hands off each other, and it had only resulted in us kissing or falling into bed.

"Listen, we're probably so worked up because we've deprived ourselves. If we give in, then we'll get over it and we can go back to being roommates," I said.

"I'm not sure if it works that way," she said.

"The other way we were trying wasn't working. I don't know about you but trying to stay away from you while living with you has been fucking terrible."

"Yeah, I know," she said. "It hasn't been fun for me either. I keep trying to tell myself to get over you."

"You can be over me. Come on up and sit on my face, love," I said, smacking her ass. She yelped.

"That's not the kind of 'over' I was talking about, Syd," she said.

"Yes, but that's the more fun kind of over," I said, sitting up and then leaning down to kiss her. "Come on, let's go get clean and then dirty and then clean again."

Lark let out a little moan as I kissed her. "We should finish talking about this."

"Later," I said. "It's time for me to get you off again."

She didn't argue with me.

～

EVENTUALLY BOTH OUR stomachs were growling, and we'd run out of hot water, so we got out of the shower and into comfortable pajamas.

"I wish we could order delivery," Lark said. "That's one thing I miss about college. Food delivery."

"I know. I keep asking Nick if he'd do limited delivery, but he always tells me it wouldn't work."

Lark searched through the cupboards while I checked the fridge and freezer.

"I have a lasagna in here that we can throw in the oven," I said, pulling the box out.

"Works for me," she said.

Layne would have been horrified to see the box of premade lasagna, but she wasn't here to judge me.

I set the oven to preheat and pulled the tray out of the box. "I must have bought this when it was on sale."

Lark came up behind me and put her arms around my waist, pressing her face into my spine.

"What are you doing?" I asked.

"You smell really good right now," she said, her voice muffled.

"Thanks?" I said. She rubbed her face into my back and I just…let her. I leaned back and felt her warm body on mine.

"You smell really good all the time," I said, shoving the lasagna in the oven.

"Thanks," she said.

I turned around and found her looking at me, her hair damp, her cheeks pink. I reached for her face and kissed her.

"What was that for?"

I shrugged. "I needed to kiss you."

She grinned at me and pulled me closer with her hands on my hips.

WE DIDN'T EVEN BOTHER to get out two plates for the lasagna. I sliced a huge piece and threw it on one plate and we sat on the couch with it like goblins. Clementine had to come and investigate, but left because, unlike another orange cat, lasagna wasn't his thing.

Lark and I lay on the couch with our plate and our legs wrapped around each other.

I couldn't remember the last time I'd been this relaxed. It had been a while.

We finished all the episodes of our show and then Lark went searching with the remote for something new.

"What about this?" she asked, stopping on a true crime documentary.

"Sounds good," I said without even reading the summary.

Lark put her fork down with a sigh and folded her hands on her belly.

Instead of watching the show, I just kept watching her. Her curls were just starting to dry, and I wanted to run my fingers through them. I wanted to lay in bed with her and ask her about every single scar on her perfect skin. I wanted to hear about her Christmases and birthdays and what she'd been like in school. I wanted to talk to her about everything and nothing.

I moved the lasagna plate onto the coffee table and wiggled

closer to her, resting my head on her chest. One of her hands went to my hair, stroking it even though it was still damp.

My eyes closed and I was asleep within minutes.

"SYD," a soft voice said. I woke up and realized that I'd had an accidental nap on Lark.

I sat up and rubbed my eyes. "Sorry."

"It's okay. I didn't want to wake you up, but I really have to pee," she said, blushing a little bit.

"No problem," I said. "I'm going to make some tea, do you want some?"

"Sure," she said, getting up and heading to the bathroom.

I stretched a little bit before I got to my feet and went to the kitchen to make tea.

Lark resumed her spot after she finished in the bathroom and I brought the tea over for both of us.

"Thanks," she said, taking it from me. Fuck, she was so pretty, I could barely stand it.

I snuggled back into her again and she put her arm around me.

"This is nice," she said.

"Yeah. I've been snuggle deprived for a long time," I said.

"I thought you didn't do snuggling," she said.

"Oh, I definitely do snuggling. It's great. Big fan," I said.

"How do you separate snuggling from the whole relation-ship thing? I'm just trying to understand," she said. My friends had asked me the same sort of thing. They'd been trying to figure me out for years, but so far, they hadn't been able to crack the mystery that was how my brain worked.

"I guess I just put sex and that sort of physical stuff in a box and then my regular life in another. People come into my life and then they go out of it. No drama, no issues. I get to do all my regular shit and then when I need sex or companion-ship, I find someone to fill that need. It works for me," I said.

Lark thought about that as she drank her tea.

"That makes sense. But you don't want anyone to stick around?"

Now I was the one who had to think about my answer. "I never have before."

That was the absolute truth. I'd never ached for more before.

"What would you do if you ever wanted someone in your life all the time?" she asked and I let myself look deep into her blue eyes.

"I'll let you know if it happens," I said.

LARK SEEMED to hesitate before heading to bed.

"What is it?" I asked, folding the blanket we'd been using and tossing it on the back of the couch.

"Nothing," she said, shaking her head. "I just...nothing."

I reached for her arm to stop her. "What is it?" I asked.

She looked down at the floor as her cheeks turned pink.

"Tell me, love," I said, running my thumb over the back of her knuckles.

"Kiss me goodnight?" she asked, not looking up at me.

"Is that what you wanted?" I asked, using my other hand to tip her chin up.

"Yeah," she said. "I know it's silly." I stopped her from saying anything else by kissing her.

"Goodnight, Lark," I said.

"Goodnight, Syd," she said back.

Chapter Eleven

THAT NIGHT I slept better than I had even during the weekend friend retreat. Satisfying sex was good for me, obviously.

I sighed happily and stretched my arms after my alarm went off. I heard Lark getting up and getting ready and I rushed to the bathroom to wash my face and brush my teeth and fix my hair. Lark had seen me in all my glory already, but for some reason I wanted to see her this morning looking fresh.

I came out of the bathroom and saw her in the kitchen making coffee and talking to Clementine.

"Is he begging?" I asked.

"Yes," she said with a laugh.

"I've got it," I said, brushing past her and sliding my hand on her back. Her hair was all over the place and she was glowing. I really, really wanted to toss her on the couch and make both of us late for work.

I took a deep breath and got my needy cat his morning wet food so he wouldn't claw me to death in my sleep.

Lark had already made my coffee and dosed it with just the right amount of creamer.

"Thanks," I said.

"You're welcome," she said, pulling herself to sit on the counter. "What are we having for breakfast?"

"Oh, I'm supposed to make breakfast for you now? Is that what's happening?" I said.

She nodded. "I'll do it tomorrow."

I sighed as if it was a big imposition. "I suppose."

"What if I kiss you?" she asked.

"A kiss for a meal? I don't know. I think I at least deserve an orgasm."

She snorted. "If you want an orgasm, you're gonna have to be fast."

Lark crooked her finger at me to come closer, so I did, kissing her as she slid her hand into my shorts. She gasped when she found me wet already as she thrust her fingers inside me and pressed her palm to my clit. I rubbed against her hand and she let me use her to fuck myself into a quick, hard climax that almost made me fall over.

Lark smirked at me as I trembled with the last little shocks as warmth washed over me.

"Okay, okay, I'll make you breakfast," I said, kissing her lips.

I went to the fridge to get out some eggs and butter and sausage and toast. I turned and caught Lark licking her fingers.

"That is so fucking hot," I said, the carton of eggs nearly sliding out of my hands.

"Couldn't help myself," she said, shrugging.

What was she doing to me?

"WHOA, you look happy. Guess your hookup went well yesterday," Joy said during lunch.

"What?" I asked. Oh, right. My failed hookup that turned into me and Lark fucking when I got back and attacked her. I opened my mouth to tell Joy about it and then slammed my jaw shut. Lark and I still hadn't even talked about what we were doing, and I didn't need anyone's opinion on it this time.

"Your hookup?" Joy said. "Because you've got a major 'I had a lot of sex' glow that I haven't seen on you in a while," she said.

"My hookup was fantastic," I said. "Incredible. Five stars."

Joy snorted and shook her head. "You going to see her again?"

"You never know," I said, which wasn't a yes or a no.

Joy studied me, her eyes narrowing. I thought she was going to call me out, but she didn't.

"Well, I'm glad to see you happy," she said. "However that happens. You deserve it."

"Thanks," I said. "You're the best, babe."

"I try," she said.

"You're very good at it," I said.

She grinned and picked up half of her sandwich.

"So, back to plans for the engagement party," she said. I put a smile on my face and tried not to groan.

I HATE **people** Lark messaged me that afternoon.

Me too. They're the worst I responded. She followed her message up with a picture of her making a face while wearing her work shirt with the logo of the coffeeshop on it. Fortunately, she didn't have to wear a nametag or a hat or anything like that even though she would have looked cute as hell in them.

I sent her a picture of all the boxes I needed to somehow get packed.

I'm just going to hire someone and see if my mom

notices. I mean, I do the payroll, so it's not like she could even stop me I sent.

Do it Lark sent.

You're a bad influence on me I responded.

Someone had just walked into the shop, so I had to abandon the box packing to see who it was.

A somewhat frazzled-looking woman stood in front of me. Her hair was lavender and pulled up in a messy bun and it somehow didn't clash with her green eyes. A pair of glasses with beige plastic frames sat on her nose.

"Can I help you?" I asked. She'd been glancing around, her lips pressed together.

"Oh, uh, hi, yes," she said, blinking a few times. "I was wondering if you're hiring?"

"We are," I said. "Are you looking for work?"

She nodded. "Yes, and I haven't had much luck."

"There aren't a whole lot of opportunities in Arrowbridge. Are you from around here?" I asked. She didn't look familiar to me.

"No. I moved here a month ago," she said, not elaborating more than that. Okay then. It was a little strange for someone to move to a new place before they secured a job, but I wasn't going to judge this stranger.

"I'm Sydney," I said, sticking my hand out.

"Everly," she said, shaking my hand.

"Pretty name," I said.

"Thanks. Are you the manager?" she asked.

"Oh, yes, I am. Did you have time for an interview right now?" The day was cloudy and cold, and there weren't a whole lot of people shopping right now.

"Yeah, I guess so?" she said.

"Or we can schedule one at another time, if you need to." She shook her head.

"No, now is good."

"Great," I said. I wasn't going to get my hopes up, but so far, Everly might be just what I was looking for.

To help her relax a little, I gave her a tour of the store and asked her if she had retail experience.

"Oh yeah," she said with a rueful smile. "I've done it all. I could sell ice in Alaska."

I liked that. She pulled a printed resume out of her purse and handed it to me.

"I know everyone does things online, but I made these just in case."

I took it from her and scanned it. Looking at her high school and college graduation dates put her at about twenty-six, twenty-seven. She was originally from Massachusetts, and I could hear the hint of an accent on certain words. I couldn't really talk, since I was sure my Maine accent came out every now and then.

"We only really have enough work for someone part time to start, but the position could move to full-time," I said. I wanted her to know that upfront.

Everly nodded. "That's fine. I'm looking to get my foot in the door somewhere."

I scanned the resume again and then put it behind the register before picking up one of the mugs. I'd never truly interviewed someone before like this, but I'd looked up some scripts and tips online.

"Pretend I'm someone who just walked into the shop. Sell me on this mug," I said, handing it to her.

Everly blinked once and then took the mug from me.

"Hello," I said, pretending to be a customer.

"Hello, welcome to Bluebird Pottery, how can I help you?" she said in a pleasant voice.

I decided to make this a little bit easier for her.

"I'm looking for a gift for a friend, but I don't know what to get for her," I said, looking around.

"Is your friend a coffee or tea drinker?" she asked.

"No, she's not," I said. I couldn't make things *too* easy.

"What kind of things does she like?" Everly asked, not deterred.

"She loves corgis," I said.

The mug I'd handed Everly had a moose on it.

"Does she have any hobbies?" Everly asked.

I sighed. "Well, she does love hiking."

"What about a mug? She doesn't have to use them for drinks. They're great for holding pens, or for spare change. And this one has the sweetest little moose on it. Each of our mugs is also handmade, so no two of them are alike," she said.

"I don't know," I said, taking the mug from her as the customer.

Everly leaned close to me as if she was going to share a secret. "Now, I don't normally do this, but how about I offer you a special discount and I'll wrap it up for her so you don't even have to worry about wrapping paper."

I smiled.

"You're hired," I said.

EVERLY WAS THRILLED and I went ahead and got her information and told her I was going to check her references, but if everything was good to go, she could come in on Wednesday for her first training shift.

I could tell she was trying to hold back her excitement as she thanked me and then walked out of the shop to do a little happy dance on the sidewalk. Cute.

"Hey Mom?" I said, going into the back.

Mom looked up from the pot she was painting. "Huh?"

"I just hired someone to help part time. You'll meet her on Wednesday."

Mom blinked at me a few times.

"Sydney, you did what?" She set down her brush.

"I hired someone to help. We have the money and I can't do everything anymore. She's really nice and I'm going to teach her everything I know," I said.

Mom sighed. "Oh Sydney. I wished you had consulted me before going ahead with this."

"I *did* consult you. I tried to get you to look at applications and set up interviews and you wouldn't, so I took matters into my own hands," I said. "I need help, Mom."

I hated saying that, but it was true. I'd been drowning in this job for a while and Everly had just thrown me a life preserver. If I had more help, then I might be able to do other projects and work on adding more products to the online store and do more marketing. Stuff I was good at. Packing boxes made me want to throw myself into the kiln.

Mom looked like she was going to argue, but then she stared into my eyes for a few seconds.

"Okay," she said. "I trust you."

"Thank you," I said. "I'm going to have her train and be on a trial basis, but I have a really good feeling about her."

"Your feelings are usually right," Mom said.

"I know," I said, and she tossed a wet paper towel ball at me.

"Modesty is a virtue," she said.

"Modesty is boring," I told her as I started wrapping a mug in tissue for shipping.

LARK MESSAGED me off and on for the rest of the day and asked me what I was doing for dinner. I guess all our meals were going to be communal now, which was easier for both of us. She said since I'd done breakfast, she could handle dinner.

I'm fine with whatever you feel like making I sent. Knowing that I didn't have to cook tonight was pretty fucking great. It was almost like having Joy living with me again, except I had never wanted to have sex with Joy.

I almost skipped up the stairs to my apartment after closing the shop for the day. I'd gotten in touch with Everly's references and they'd all been completely glowing and said that I would be a fool not to hire her. They might have just been her friends pretending to talk her up, but I didn't think so.

Lark wasn't home yet, but I went ahead and unloaded the dishwasher and fed Clementine before sitting down to read until she got home.

"Hey," Lark said, pushing through the door and hauling several bags of groceries.

"Whoa, need some help?" I asked.

"No, I've got it," she said, hauling the bags up and setting them on the counter with a grunt.

"You know we have food," I said.

"I know, but we were out of some stuff," she said, staring to put things away.

She paused and came over to give me a kiss. Her lips were cold from being outside.

"Hello," she said.

"Hello. What are we having for dinner?" I asked.

"I was absolutely craving white chicken chili, so I found a recipe online and I'm going to hope that I don't mess it up," Lark said, pulling out some peppers and setting them on the counter.

"That sounds seriously amazing," I said.

"I didn't get the hottest chilis, so you'll just have to add your sauce to make yours the right heat level," she said.

"That's fine. I'm used to it," I said.

I could go back to my book, but I sat at one of the stools

and talked to Lark as she made dinner and Clementine begged for scraps.

"This would burn your little whiskers," Lark told him while she sliced the peppers and removed the seeds.

"Let him sniff one and see how he reacts," I said. Lark picked up one of the peppers she'd sliced in half and held it in front of his face. He recoiled instantly and glared at her with betrayal in his eyes.

"I told you, silly boy," Lark said.

A few seconds later, Clementine was begging again, as if nothing had happened.

"His brain isn't the brainiest," I said. "It's okay, we still love him."

"Yes we do," Lark said.

"Oh, I forgot to tell you that I hired someone today."

Lark paused in slicing the peppers. "That's amazing, how did that happen?"

"Honestly, she walked in and asked for a job and I interviewed her on the spot and she's coming in on Wednesday to train."

"That almost seems like it was meant to be," she said, finishing up the peppers and throwing them in the pot.

"I know. I'm trying not to get my hopes up. This could absolutely bite me in the ass. I've never hired anyone before," I said.

"I'm sure it will be fine. You checked her references and so forth, right?" I nodded. "I even ran her name through court records just in case. I mean, not that I'm going to turn someone away who had an arrest record, but I just wanted to make sure there wasn't like, a long history of embezzlement or something."

Talking to Lark was so easy. She'd gone from this person I'd fucked once to this woman that I could shoot the shit with over just about anything.

The white chicken chili was completely delicious, and I couldn't stop eating it, even after I was full.

"I made enough so we'll have leftovers," she said.

After, we tangled ourselves on the couch as Lark watched random videos and I read a book.

Things between us were…comfortable. Easy. As if they always should have been like this. Both of us had been fighting this, and for what?

Lark let out a little sigh and I looked up from my book.

"I think I'm going to take a bath," she said. I moved my legs so she could get up. "You want to join me?"

"Will we both fit in the tub?" I asked.

Lark laughed. "Let's find out."

TURNED out that you could fit two people in our tub, but barely. Trying to cram both of us without sloshing too much water on the floor wasn't easy, but we did our best and I just mopped up the floor after.

Lark took a shower to wash her hair and I went after. When I came out, she was on the couch as if she was waiting for me.

"Going to bed?" I asked.

"In a little bit," she said. I blotted my hair with my towel and sat down on the couch with my comb.

"Turn around," Lark said.

"Oh, you don't have to do that," I said.

"It's the least I can do since you took care of me while I was sick, and while I was hung over. I've got to make up for that somehow," she said, and I felt her hands working some of my styling cream through the ends of my hair before she took my brush and started gently on the ends and working her way up.

Lark was gentle, even when she hit a snag, and I relaxed into the soothing motions of the brush.

When she was done, she worked her fingers into my scalp as a little massage and I couldn't help but moan.

"That feels so good," I said, my eyes half closed.

Lark brushed through my hair one last time and then I felt her lips on the top of my head as she pulled it back.

"Thank you," I said, turning to face her.

"You have gorgeous hair," she said. "I'm so jealous."

What?

"You literally look like a hair model all the time, what are you talking about?" I said.

Lark rolled her eyes. "It definitely does not look great all the time. You should see me in the humidity. It's frizz city."

"Lark, you're gorgeous. You're always gorgeous. You're so pretty that I forget what the hell I'm doing sometimes," I said.

She blushed. "That's flattering."

"It's not flattering, it's just the truth. Things would be a lot easier for me if you were less attractive," I admitted.

She laughed. "Okay, I'll do my best to be less attractive."

I put my hand under her chin and kissed her. "Don't. I like looking at you."

Lark pulled back from the kiss and looked into my eyes.

"We should go to bed," she said.

"Yours or mine?" I said before I could think about whether that was a good idea or not.

"Separately," she said. "I think we should have our own rooms at night."

Well that was no fun, but it did make sense.

I blew out a frustrated breath. "Okay. Then one more kiss."

I kissed her and slipped my tongue into her mouth. When I pulled back, she had a dazed look in her eyes, and I wasn't so steady myself.

"Goodnight, Lark," I said, standing on shaky legs.

"Night," she said, still staring off into space.

For a second, I considered going back to kiss her again, but I forced myself to go to my room and shut the door. She headed to her room a few minutes later, shutting the door firmly.

EVERLY SHOWED up fifteen minutes early for her training session on Wednesday. I was back to having trouble sleeping, so I wasn't at my best, but I tried to give her a smile as I sucked down another cup of coffee so I wouldn't fall asleep while standing up.

While I took her around the shop again and gave her a more detailed tour, she took notes in a notebook, and I realized just how petite she was. She had so much energy that seemed taller at first.

"Don't worry, I'm not going to quiz you," I joked as we made it back to the register.

"You could. I'm going to learn this all, I promise," she said, writing something else down. She seemed serious.

"Okay, so you should probably meet my mom, a.k.a., the reason all of this exists," I said, waving around the shop.

"Great," Everly said, tucking a strand of purple hair behind her ear. She had a whole lot of silver piercings in one of her small ears.

I led her into the back, hoping that Mom would be normal and wouldn't scare her away. There was a reason I'd been putting off this introduction.

"Mom?" I called. She came out of the supply closet and smiled.

"This is Everly, our new employee," I said, gesturing to Everly.

"Everly, this is the founder and creator of Bluebird Pottery, Eileen Sparks," I said.

"It's a pleasure to meet you," Everly said, sticking her hand out. Mom tried to wipe hers on her apron, but that didn't do a whole lot to get the clay and glaze off her hands.

"Nice to meet you, Everly," Mom said, and I knew she was absolutely going to forget Everly's name at least five hundred times. "Sorry about that."

Everly wiped her hand on her jeans. "No worries."

She smiled and looked around the room. "I feel like I don't know how a lot of pottery is made. I remember making little clay bowls in art class, but nothing like this." She edged toward the pottery wheel and Mom gave me a look before walking over and explaining her process to Everly, who did seem interested to learn.

After a few moments of making sure they were good together, I left them to head out to the front in case a customer came in.

A few seconds later, I heard laughter, so I guess it was going well.

The door rang and a few people came in, so I was busy with that for a while, and then we had a mini rush. When I next checked on Everly and Mom, Everly was asking a question about something and Mom was explaining her process, her hands flying everywhere and her eyes bright.

"How's it going back here?" I asked.

"Good," they both said at the same time and laughed.

"Just let me know when you're ready to start learning the POS system, Everly," I said.

"I will," she said, and went back to listening to Mom. Yeah, she was going to work out just fine.

Chapter Twelve

LARK AND I fumbled through the rest of the work week together. I didn't know what we were supposed to be doing, but what we ended up doing was cooking for each other, snuggling on the couch until we started to make out and then fuck, and then took a shower after. I asked her to brush my hair out because it was much nicer than doing it myself. She even sang a little bit more for me, which I cherished since I knew she was so shy about sharing her voice.

Every night I'd give her a kiss and go to my room and lay there, telling myself that I shouldn't just push through her door and crawl into bed with her. Lark had set that boundary, and I was going to respect that one, at least.

Joy came over on Saturday to talk about engagement party logistics, and Lark invited Mia over. They went into Lark's room, and I could not focus on what Joy was saying to me.

I had never seen a spark or anything that indicated either Lark or Mia were interested in each other, but you never knew.

"Syd, are you even listening to me?" Joy asked, snapping her fingers in front of my face.

"Yes, I am," I said, moving my eyes from Lark's door to Joy's face.

"What did I just say?" she asked, crossing her arms.

"Something about decorations," I said.

Joy huffed. "What specifically did I say about decorations?"

"Colors?" I guessed.

"Syd, what is up with you? You're completely distracted and I'm going to take a shot in the dark and guess it's behind door number one," she said, pointing to her former room.

"No, it's not," I said too quickly.

"You're jealous," she said with a smirk. "It looks good on you."

"I'm not jealous," I said. "I'm just…"

"Jealous," Joy sang. "It's okay, we've all been there."

"I'm not jealous," I said, and cringed at how petulant my voice sounded in my own ears.

"Joy. It's okay to have feelings for someone. We've talked about this." She put her hand on mine, which had curled into a fist.

"I don't have feelings for her. I like hanging out with her. That's it," I said.

Joy sighed. "You're stubborn as hell, you know that?"

"Yes, I've been told," I said, grinning at her.

Lark's door opened and I jumped. Mia came out and waved before heading into the bathroom.

"You are so jealous," Joy said. She sounded thrilled.

"Am not," I said.

JOY HEADED BACK to her apartment to have dinner with her love, and Mia decided to stick around with us.

"I'm still living at home, so anytime I can get out is much

appreciated," she said as we crammed on the couch. She took the furthest spot on the left side with Lark in the middle.

Tonight, Lark had been in charge of cooking, and had used one of Layne's recipes to make the most delicious orange chicken with rice and veggies.

I did my best not to glare at Mia whenever she spoke and did my best to ask her questions about her life. If she was going to be around, I might as well get to know her. From everything I'd seen, she was a sweet and bubbly person, and a good friend to Lark. That didn't mean I wasn't going to lose my shit when they went into Lark's room together and closed the door.

"I can't wait for book club," Mia said. "I hope I have something to contribute."

"Don't worry about that. You only have to talk if you want to," Lark said. "Right, Sydney?"

"Right," I said, nodding.

I clenched my teeth. Why did this nice girl joining book club set me on edge? I needed to get my shit together.

Somehow, I got through dinner and then Mia and Lark decided they wanted to watch a movie. I should have gone to my room and tried to read a book, but I wanted to keep my eye on them to see if there was any kind of sexual tension between them. So far, I hadn't seen any, but you never knew when attraction could strike. I was on the lookout.

After what seemed like forever, Mia said she should probably get home and I said goodnight and Lark walked her to the door.

"What the hell is wrong with you?" Lark asked once Mia was gone.

"What?" I asked, peering over the back of the couch.

"You were being so fucking weird, Sydney. Mia was being super nice, and you kept staring at her like she was going to rob you," she said, coming over and flopping in the space Mia had just vacated.

"I wasn't being weird," I said. I'd been perfectly pleasant to her. I'd made small talk!

"You were. The irritation was radiating off you," she said. "Is there something wrong with Mia?"

"No," I said. "I don't know why you think I was irritated, but I wasn't. Must have been my resting bitch face." That had been the culprit before of people thinking I was upset or pissed when I wasn't.

"It was your whole energy," Lark said, pointing at me. "If there's nothing wrong with Mia, then why were you giving her the stink eye the whole time?"

"I wasn't!" I got up from the couch and started pacing. "I wasn't giving her the stink eye."

Lark watched me pace for a few seconds and then her face lit up.

"Wait. Are you jealous?"

I froze and turned around to face her.

"No, I'm not jealous! Fuck. I'm fine, everything is fine!" I threw my hands in the air and wanted to scream again, but that would just alarm the neighbors.

"Syd. It's okay to be jealous," Lark said softly, getting up from the couch.

I wanted to argue with her, but I didn't know what else to say. She laughed softly and put her arms around me.

"It's cute that you're jealous," she said. I hesitated a second before I put my arms around her and buried my face in her hair. She always smelled so damn good.

"I'm not jealous," I said, my voice muffled into her shoulder.

"Okay, you're not jealous, but you're definitely something. Poor Mia."

I made a grumbling noise.

"So grumpy," Lark said, pulling back and smiling at me. "It's okay. Be grumpy if you want to."

She tucked my hair behind my ears and then kissed the tip of my nose.

I melted into her arms again and sighed. "I'm not grumpy."

Lark laughed and kissed me. "I know what to do to take care of your grumps."

I gazed into her eyes. "Does it involve you getting naked?"

She nodded. "Nudity is definitely involved."

LARK AND I were in bed for so long, and so tired after our shower that I just followed her to bed and collapsed on her mattress in my towel.

"Move over," she said, trying to roll me to make space. I did what I could and rested back against her pillows.

"Sleep now," I said.

Lark shoved at me half-heartedly. "You have your own bed for that."

"Yours is nicer," I said, nuzzling into her pillows and inhaling her scent.

"Sydney, come on," she said. I rolled over and opened my eyes to look at her.

"Please?" I asked.

She leaned down to kiss me. "Okay. But just for tonight."

"Yay," I said and then yawned.

"Give me your towel," she said. I tried to yank the towel out from under me, but it didn't really work.

Lark laughed. "You tired burrito."

I started humming.

"What is that?" she asked, taking one end of the towel and then pushing my shoulder so I rolled off the rest of it.

"I was making burrito noises," I said.

Lark finally got the towel away from me and I was naked in the bed.

"Night night," I said.

"Get under the covers, Syd," Lark said as she put on her pajamas.

I slid between her sheets and sighed happily.

"You're very naked right now," she said as she got in next to me and turned to face me. I could barely keep my eyes open.

I made more humming noises.

Lark laughed and rested her head on my shoulder. "You're too tired to take advantage of right now, my cute burrito."

"Mmmm," I said, closing my eyes completely. Her lips met mine briefly.

"Go to sleep, burrito."

∾

WHEN I WOKE naked in Lark's bed, I was very confused for a few seconds. I blinked and looked over at her body curled into mine. She was still out, her face soft in sleep.

Trying not to feel like a creep, I watched her and stroked her curls as she rested so close to me.

I jumped as the alarm on Lark's phone went off. She reached over and slapped it to make it stop. Her eyes opened and she looked up at me.

"Good morning," she said, her voice rough. "Sorry, I forgot to turn my alarm off last night."

"Good morning," I said, unable to stop the urge to kiss her, so I did.

Lark smiled at me. "What are we having for breakfast?"

"Whatever you want," I said.

∾

LARK AND I lazed in bed for a little while before getting up and heading to the kitchen in search of food and caffeine. I'd gone to my room to grab some sweatpants and a shirt since cooking naked was dangerous.

"How about I help you with breakfast today?" Lark asked, kissing the back of my neck. I completely forgot what I was doing as her tongue drew little designs on my skin.

"What?" I asked.

She chuckled and before I knew what was happening, her hand was sliding into the front of my sweatpants, making a little satisfied sound to find me wet already. I'd woken up unbearably horny, as usual. I was just getting used to being ready to go at any second when I was around her. My sex drive seemed to have gone up, not down, the longer I'd lived with her. It was a good thing I didn't have a penis or else I'd just have a constant boner walking around everywhere.

"Mmmm," she said, circling my clit with her fingers. "What a sweet little burrito."

Her words cut through my lust haze. "Are you referring to my junk as a burrito now?"

"Well, I am going to stuff it, so sure," she said, and my horny brain was both confused and hungry at the same time.

"I don't know why this is working for me, but it is," I said, and she plunged three fingers inside me with no prep, but I was ready for her. Both hands went to the counter to hold me up so I didn't completely collapse to the floor.

Lark fucked me slowly, and it was maddening.

"Please, Lark, please," I said, trying to push myself against her for more sensation.

"Shh, it's okay love," she said, using her other hand to clasp one of my nipples and roll it between her fingers.

I gasped and trembled before I clamped my hand around her wrist and forcing her to go faster. She didn't stop me, just let me use her as she curled her fingers inside me, setting off a toe-curling orgasm that almost had me folding to the floor, but Lark managed to hold me up as my body convulsed with each wave of pleasure.

Lark stroked my hair and waited with me for the storm to be over. Eventually I let go of her wrist and braced myself on the counter.

"Fucking hell, Lark," I said, still shaking in the aftermath. My body folded over the counter and I pressed my heated cheek to the cool surface.

Lark laughed and patted me on the back.

"Good morning, Syd."

OF COURSE, I had to get her back before we had breakfast, so before I could even decide what we were going to eat, I told her to get on the counter and spread her legs so I could make her come with my mouth and my fingers. It took all of a few minutes to have her screaming.

"I love the way your burrito tastes," I said, licking my lips afterward.

Lark giggled. "I don't know how far we can carry this metaphor until it gets weird."

"Let's find out," I said, helping her down.

Lark sliced strawberries while I minded the chocolate chip pancakes in the pan and the bacon on a tray in the oven. She hummed a random song softly and I kept getting distracted by her and almost burned the pancakes several times.

"We have to have whipped cream," Lark said, pulling a can out of the fridge and brandishing it at me.

"Oh, absolutely," I said. "You can have as much as you want."

Lark absolutely covered her pancakes until you couldn't even see them anymore.

"My mother never let me do things like this, so getting to do them as an adult makes me happy," she said, sprinkling sliced strawberries on top of her whipped cream pancakes.

I put my hands on her shoulders and turned her to face me.

"You deserve whipped cream," I said slowly. "If you want drums of whipped cream, you should have them."

Lark laughed. "I don't think I need that much whipped cream. But I like the sentiment anyway."

She leaned forward to kiss me. "Thank you."

"You're welcome."

"SHOULD WE DO SOMETHING TODAY?" she asked. "I feel like I've only gone to work and then come home."

We'd finished our breakfast and were just wrapped around each other on the couch, as usual.

"We could go on a book crawl," I said.

"What's that?" I was surprised Layne or Honor hadn't told her about it.

"It's like a pub crawl, but we go to different bookstores and buy a book at each one. I can't remember if Layne or Joy came up with it, but we do it every time we go on a trip. Except for the last trip, because we were in the middle of fucking nowhere." The cabin had been nice, but there was a distinct lack of civilization.

Lark sat up, her blue eyes bright. "That sounds fun, can we do it?"

I ran my fingers through her hair. "We can do whatever you want, my little burrito."

I WASN'T USUALLY the planner for things like the book crawl, so Lark decided she wanted to plan our route. The destinations weren't important to me, and the books were almost superfluous to spending time with Lark. Since she was deciding where we were going, I agreed to drive. The forecast was clear with zero snow or rain, so it was a perfect day for a drive.

I packed up my bag with snacks and drinks for the road and Lark bounced over when she was ready.

"You are very excited about this trip," I said.

"It's our first roommate road trip," she said, and for some reason, the word "roommate" made my stomach churn a little bit. I'd probably eaten too many pancakes.

"Let's go," I said, taking her hand.

LARK WAS the perfect road trip companion. She let me be in charge of what we listened to, she told me when the turns were coming up, even ahead of the GPS, and she always said something interesting. As a bonus, she held the snack bags open for me so I could eat with one hand and keep driving.

Our first stop was a store I'd been to before but was one of my favorites. Located in a brick building in a town about twenty minutes away from Arrowbridge, it had an odd and eclectic selection, with a weirdly high amount of true crime about women murdering their husbands. Didn't know what that was about, but they had a great cozy mystery section, so I was happy.

"Okay, help me find a book," Lark said as we got out of the car after parking at a meter down the street from the shop.

"We'll find you a book, don't worry," I said as I fed the meter and made sure my car was locked. Lark skipped onto the sidewalk and then took my gloved hand in hers, swinging our arms together.

I thought back and couldn't remember ever holding hands with someone like this. At least not someone that I'd slept with. I might have held Joy or Layne's hand to be funny, never like this.

Lark chattered away, telling me about her book selecting process as she kept swinging our hands together.

She had no idea that thoughts were completely exploding in my brain.

Holding hands with Lark as we walked down the street was... I loved it. Even though I couldn't feel her skin against mine, the warmth of her hand washed over me and I couldn't stop smiling.

She held the door for me, and we walked into the three-story shop. The space was cramped, but that was all part of the charm.

Lark went for the bestseller table first, and I was just along for the ride. I let her drag me up and down each floor, trying to decide what she was going to get. I even grabbed a basket to carry around her potential selections. Lark seemed to want options before she made her final choice.

By the time we'd made it through all the shelves, she had five potential selections in her basket. I'd picked up the first two cozy mysteries from a new-to-me author, so I was set.

"Okay," Lark said as we sat at a table in the small café on the second floor. She held up the first choice, a non-fiction book about someone who had escaped a religious cult.

I sat back and watched her hold up each book and read the blurb, then set it aside and pick up the next one. At last, she settled on a romance book, a classic sapphic romance from years ago that Joy had forced me to read, and which I'd loved. Obviously.

"It's a classic," I said.

"I read the other one and saw the movie. Fingers crossed this one is good too." She pointed at the title on the book.

"Haha," I said. "Cute."

"Now that I've selected my book, I need a snack," she said.

"Perfect timing that we're in a café," I said, pointing to the counter.

"Hungry?" she asked, and I nodded.

As we waited in line, she took my hand and then I leaned in to say something in her ear.

"They have burritos," I said.

She leaned back against me and I felt a little shiver go up her spine. "I saw that. I'd rather have yours right now."

I laughed. A burrito might not be the sexiest metaphor, but I liked it anyway.

Lark did not order a burrito, and instead got a fruit, nut, and cheese plate, along with a caramel latte. I got an everything bagel with cream cheese and an iced coffee with cream and sugar.

"Now I feel bad that I have to give these books back and they have to reshelve them," Lark said when we got our orders and sat down at the table again.

"It's okay. At least you didn't chuck them on the floor or try to shove them back yourself. Joy always says that she wishes people would give her the books instead of trying to put them back themselves," I said.

"That makes sense," she said, reaching out and swiping her finger along my chin before licking it off.

"Cream cheese," she said with a wink.

Fuck, she was so pretty.

LARK BOUGHT her book and we headed back to the car and to our second stop, which actually was a department store that had a decent book section.

"Okay, I also needed some other stuff," she said, getting a small cart. "So that's why we're here."

We threw our bags in the cart and Lark wandered through the aisles, putting this and that in the cart, occasionally checking the list on her phone.

While we were here, I figured I could stock up on a few things, so I tossed deodorant and an air freshener and some tortillas, rice, and beans as well.

"I saw that," Lark said.

"I've got burritos on the brain," I said, leaning close and grabbing her ass. She yelped and then giggled. We earned a stern look from a woman who had to be at least a thousand years old. What was this, a library? I just gave her what I hoped was a dazzling smile and she muttered something to herself as she pushed her cart down the next aisle.

The cart had a lot of stuff in it by the time we made it to the books. Right next to the book section was an endcap with goofy gifts.

"Oh my god. We have to buy this," Lark said, holding up a box. It turned out to be a blanket that was printed and shaped to look like a tortilla.

"It's a burrito blanket," Lark said, shoving one of them at me. "We're both getting one."

I snorted as I tossed one of the blankets in the cart and Lark tossed in a second one.

"Get another one," I said. "For Clementine. Or guests."

"We couldn't leave out Clementine," Lark said, adding another blanket.

She danced along to a song as I pushed the cart into the book aisle and I reached for her.

"Come here," I said as she continued to dance, making me sway with her as I gathered her in my arms.

"What is it?" she asked, still moving. I matched my movements to hers.

"Nothing," I said, leaning in and kissing her right in the book aisle. "Just had to kiss you right here in the book aisle."

"Good place to kiss," she said.

"Mmmmm," I said.

THE BOOK SECTION at the department store mostly had bestsellers, so we caved and each got the same book, mostly to see what the hype was all about.

"I don't know," I said as Lark set two copies in the cart. "This book better not suck, hardcovers are not cheap."

"We can always donate them if we hate it," Lark said, looking over some of the other titles, and picked up a classic cookbook and added that to the stack.

"You know you can get recipes online for free," I told her.

"I know, but I like the idea of owning a cookbook. Plus, there aren't any of those annoying personal stories that you have to scroll through before you even get to the ingredients list." She rolled her eyes and I had to agree. I knew that they wrote them so people wouldn't steal their recipes, and to help with SEO, but I always got angry every time there wasn't a "jump to recipe" button to hit.

The two of us wandered through the department store, looking at shoes and clothes and finally ended up in the house-wares section.

"Why is this shit so expensive?" I said, putting a cute pillow back on the shelf after looking at the price tag.

"You never think about stuff like buying trash cans and lamps and small appliances when you're a kid thinking about what it's going to be like to be an adult. Of course, if my mother had gotten her way, I wouldn't be caught dead buying any of this because I'd have an old rich man to buy me designer trash cans for the bathroom," Lark said, making a face. "Sorry if I keep bringing her up."

"Hey," I said, taking her hand and kissing her palm. "It's okay. You're processing a lot of shit. Parent stuff is complicated."

"Thanks," she said. "Okay, enough of that shit." She shook her head and moved on to look at the shower curtains but didn't drop my hand.

By the time we checked out, it was getting dark, and I didn't think we were going to make it to the third location. We'd spent a lot of time at the department store.

"Are you okay if we go have dinner?" Lark asked. "The other bookstore closes in a few minutes and it's too far to make it."

"Sure," I said, adjusting her hat before we went outside.

"Is it weird that I'm totally craving Mexican right now?" she asked as we pushed the cart to my car.

"I am too. I'd kill for a burrito right now." I wiggled my eyebrows.

Lark threw back her head and let out a loud laugh that was so beautiful and bright that it made my heart feel tight in my chest.

LARK MANAGED to find a Mexican place nearby that also had bottomless margaritas.

"That is a bad idea, but maybe we could stop and get the ingredients and make them at home," Lark said.

"That is a perfect idea, let's do it."

The restaurant was completely tacky and over decorated, but the burritos were massive and delicious and the chips and salsa they brought to the table seemed to be endless, so we were happy.

"Ask for an extra box," Lark said just as the server came to see how we were doing. I still had a third of my burrito left, and Lark had only gotten through half of hers.

"Yeah, we're going to need three boxes," I said. The server nodded and grabbed them for us.

Lark glanced around a few times before dumping the tortilla chips and the little cup of salsa into the third box and closing it.

"Smart," I told her.

"I didn't want it to go to waste," she said.

This time Lark fought me for the check, and she won.

By the time we got home with our books and bags and ingredients for margaritas, I was almost too tired to make them.

Lark seemed to have more energy than I did, so she was the one who pulled out the blender and got the drinks going while I collapsed on the couch with Clementine and one of my new books.

"Your margarita, ma'am," she said, handing me a glass that was almost too full.

I took it from her, being careful not to spill. She sat down next to me with a sigh and kicked her feet up on the coffee table.

"Perfect book crawl," she said, holding her drink toward me.

Very carefully, I touched my glass to hers. "Perfect book crawl," I echoed.

Lark drank her margarita too fast and grimaced with a brain freeze.

"Slow down there," I told her, sipping mine more moderately.

"I'm good," Lark said, massaging her forehead and then draining the glass before snuggling next to me.

"I like doing random things with you," she said as she let

out a little sigh. More interested in her than my drink, I set it aside and put my arms around her.

I liked doing everything with her, but I didn't say that out loud. Instead I played with her hair and basked in the feel of her in my arms.

"Thanks for letting me live here," she said in a soft voice a few minutes later.

"Thanks for moving in," I said.

"I will deny that I said this, but I'm almost glad that the chicken house burned down. I'm not glad for Lorna, but she had insurance on it, and she honestly didn't seem that upset about it. She used the payout to buy this upscale chicken coop."

I snorted. That sounded exactly like something she would do.

"Remind me that we should go over there and get some eggs," I said.

"Good idea. I'll ask Layne if she can teach me how to make quiche."

"Fuck, I love quiche," I said.

"Speaking of quiche," Lark said, getting up and going to the pile of bags that we'd set near the door.

She pulled the burrito blankets out and held them up.

"How is that speaking of quiche?" I asked as she started ripping into the packages.

"Quiche, tortillas, there's a connection," she said, tossing one of the blankets at me. I put my hand out so it didn't hit me in the face.

Lark rejoined me and unfurled her blanket dramatically before wrapping it around herself.

"How do I look?" she asked.

"Fucking adorable," I said. She giggled and climbed onto my lap.

"Mmmmm mmm mmmmm mmmmmm," she said.

"More burrito noises?" I asked.

She nodded and leaned down to kiss me.

I gasped into her mouth and she pressed her hips into mine.

"Come on," she said. "Let's go to bed."

"Just for sex, or is sleeping involved?" I asked.

Lark snorted. "I guess you can sleep with me. For tonight."

That was exactly what she said last night, but I wasn't going to remind her and change her mind.

"Let me grab some pjs," I said as she got up, still wrapped in the blanket.

"Meet you in there," she said, pointing in the direction of her room.

I gathered some pajamas and a few other things I thought I might need if I wasn't going to be in my room for the night. I also added a few snacks and drinks to my armful and then knocked on her door with my foot.

"Whoa, are you camping out for a week?" Lark said from her bed. I couldn't answer her mostly due to the fact that she was still wrapped in the burrito blanket, but she was clearly naked underneath it.

"Is this sexy or weird?" she asked after a few seconds of silence.

I set my armful of stuff on her dresser.

"I'm going to have to say both?"

Lark sat up and the blanket slipped off her shoulder. Yup, sexy and weird, but it was absolutely working for me.

I climbed onto the bed and unwrapped her immediately, kissing my way down her body as she alternated gasps and giggles.

"Mmmmm," I said as I dipped my tongue into her navel. "Tasty."

Her knees fell open and she raised her hips, as if to draw my attention to another area of her body.

"Do you want me to taste you here?" I asked, fluttering my fingers at her entrance.

"Syd, please," she said, digging her fingers into my scalp.

"I've got you, Lark. I've got you," I said, licking a trail down her lower belly, stopping only to place kisses on each of her hips. Impatient with this tenderness, Lark just kept pushing my head lower as her legs trembled.

I fucking loved how much she needed me. Needed my body to satisfy hers.

"I've got you Lark," I said once more just before I closed my lips over her clit.

EVERLY HAD ONLY WORKED for me for less than a week, but I already didn't know how I would go back to living without her. Not only did she have a knack with customers, but she could pack a box like she'd been doing it her whole life. A lot of people might not think that was a skill, but when you were trying to ship fragile items that needed to get to their destination in one piece, it was a gift.

"Sorcery," I said as I watched her pack up a lamp. Since we were only doing mugs right now, I wanted to do a test run with a few other items and ship them to Layne and see how they fared. I wished we could do a test to send them to another state, but this was the best I could do right now.

"Thanks," Everly said. Mom came over and gave her approval.

"You're a treasure," Mom said to Everly. It had taken less than two days for Mom to completely adore her. More magic. Mom was picky about people, and she didn't make connections easily, but she chatted with Everly as she worked and I caught them laughing together all the time.

"Thank you," Everly said, cheeks growing pink.

She taped up the box and pushed her glasses up on her nose.

"I'll take this over to the post office with the others," she said, loading the box into the cart I used when I used to go do the shipping.

"Bless you," I said, and I meant it.

"Be back soon," she said as she headed out the back door.

"I love her," Mom said after the door clicked.

"I know. That's why I hired her," I said.

Mom hugged me and I inhaled the scents of clay and glaze and just a hint of her favorite rose perfume.

"Thank you," Mom said.

"You're welcome," I said, hugging her back. Mom rubbed my back and it was nice to be comforted by her instead of it being the other way around. I was so used to taking on the adult role in my relationship with her, but I tried not to think about that too much. At least I hadn't had a mother like Lark. I had never doubted, for a second, that my mom loved me and would drop everything to help me, no matter what. I'd definitely given her a few gray hairs in high school, but she'd taken it all in stride and I'd turned out okay. For the most part.

"Love you, Mom," I said before letting go of her.

"Love you, baby," Mom said, pulling back to kiss me on my forehead.

Chapter Thirteen

EVERLY CAME BACK after shipping the boxes and asked if she could rearrange some of the displays.

"Go for it," I told her, curious to see what she would come up with. A few customers drifted in and out, and I finished my bookkeeping tasks for the day, which had me ahead of schedule.

"Did you do anything fun this weekend?" I asked. I'd been doing my best to try and get to know her. It also filled the time when the shop was empty.

"Not really," she said, shrugging one shoulder as she stepped back from a shelf and then moved a stack of plates a few inches. "You?" she asked.

"Yeah, same. I did go on a book crawl with my roommate though." The word "roommate" felt wrong when it referred to Lark.

"What's a book crawl?" she asked, and I told her.

"That sounds amazing. I'm not much of a drinker myself, so buying a bunch of books is much more my speed," she said.

"That reminds me, if you ever want to join a book club,

there's one at Mainely Books once a month and we're always open for new members," I said.

"Thanks," Everly said, and that was it. Okay then. There was a cageyness about her that I couldn't figure out yet.

I left her alone after that, until she called me over to see what she'd done.

"I thought it would be good to show how it would look all together," she said, showing me the plates that she'd stacked together, along with a mug.

"It would be better with silverware and a glass and maybe a placemat," she said.

I thought about that for a second. "I'd love to do consignment pieces from local people, but I just don't think it's right for us, so I'll order some online."

"You should get a few so we can change them out with the seasons," she said.

"Smart," I said. "I'm so glad I hired you."

She smiled at me and nodded. "Me too. I know I was kind of desperate for a job, but I'm really glad I have this one."

Something fell and broke in the studio and I heard my mom cursing. I went to go deal with it, but Everly put her hand on my arm.

"I've got this," she said.

Was it too early to give her a raise?

"I KNOW that I shouldn't start relying on her, but she's made my life infinitely better," I said to Lark that night as I made spicy peanut noodles with chicken and vegetables.

Lark made a non-committal sound as she sat on one of the stools with Clementine in her lap.

I glanced up from the stove and she was staring into space.

"Lark?" I asked.

"Yeah," she said, her eyes flicking over at me. Something was off, and I wasn't going to ignore it, so I turned the burners down and went over to her.

"What's up?" I asked.

"Nothing," she said, her tone a little defensive.

I put one hand under her chin and forced her to meet my eyes. "Hey, talk to me."

"Is she pretty?" she said after a few seconds of hesitation.

"Is who pretty?" I asked.

"Everly. Is she pretty?" I blinked at her. Why was she...

Oh.

I held Lark's face between my hands and kissed her forehead. "Not even close to as pretty as you."

Lark scoffed. "You're just saying that."

"No, I'm not. I don't bullshit compliments like that. She's not my type. And she's my employee. I'd never cross that boundary even if I was attracted to her. Which I'm not. You have nothing to worry about, my anxious burrito."

Lark kissed my mouth. "See? I have no problem admitting jealousy."

"You didn't admit it right away, and I wasn't jealous of Mia," I said.

"Agree to disagree," she said, and I had to rush over and make sure the chicken didn't burn.

"If you really want to meet Everly, I can probably arrange that. She's a bit shy around new people, and I don't know her that well yet, but I'm going to try and see if she'll come to book club," I said, turning the chicken.

"I'm not that paranoid," she said. "But I would like to meet her, since she's a part of your life now."

"She's fun. An interesting combination of bubbly and reserved. I still don't know much personal information about her, apart from what she gave me so I could pay her and the little things she's told me," I said.

"Mysterious. I wonder what brought her here if she didn't have work yet," she said.

I shook my head as I carried the pot of noodles to the sink to drain. "No idea. I'm sure it's something like a sick relative that she just doesn't want to talk about because it's painful."

"Makes sense," Lark said. "You should tell her to go to the bookstore when Joy is there."

That was actually a good idea. Everyone felt comfortable with Joy. She just had such an open, comforting personality. No one could hold up for long with her. Even the grumpiest grump would end up smiling by the end of a chat with Joy.

I pulled out my phone and sent a message to Joy asking her if she could swing by the store and pretend that she had to come there for a reason so I could introduce her to Everly. She'd been dying for this invitation, so she immediately said that she would be there.

"Done. She'll be best friends with Joy within a week, just you watch. And as soon as she meets Layne, it will all be over. If they decide they want to be friends with you, there's not a whole lot you can do about it."

Lark laughed. "Yeah, I didn't exactly intend to join this little group, but my sister brought me along for the ride."

I gasped dramatically, pretending to be offended. "Are you saying you wouldn't have chosen us?"

She got off her stool and came over to me, putting her arms on my shoulders.

"I don't know if I would have chosen you. But I'm choosing you now," she said, kissing me. My hands gripped her waist, fingers sliding under her shirt in search of her warm skin.

"I choose you too," I said, resting my forehead against hers. "I'm so glad I didn't have to invite a stranger to move in here. You saved me."

Lark looked into my eyes and I almost wanted to look away

from the intensity I found there. "From having to find another roommate," I added. "You saved me from living with a weirdo."

She studied me for a few moments. "You're welcome," she said, stepping away from me.

AFTER DINNER, we took a bath again and then fucked slowly in her bed, and this time I brought out my harness. I didn't use it with every partner, but I had it on hand, just in case.

"What do you think?" I said, holding up the harness and one of my dildos. The new purple sparkly one I'd bought before she moved in.

Lark's eyes lit up immediately and her skin flushed. That was all I needed to see.

I set the harness and dildo down on the bed and crawled toward her. "Do you want me to top, or do you?"

Lark looked at the harness and then back at me.

"Can I try it? I've never worn one before."

This was my absolute favorite thing: helping one of my partners try something new with me.

"Of course you can," I said. "We'll just have to adjust it for you. Stand up."

We were both already naked, so I helped her put her legs into the harness loops and pull it up.

"How does that feel?" I asked as I made sure it fit her and wasn't going to fall off in the midst of fucking. That was no fun. Almost as bad as having your vibrator battery die just as you were about to come.

Lark's eyelashes fluttered as if she was already turned on and she hadn't even added the dildo.

"Good," she said, her pupils blown.

I held back a laugh as I helped her add the dildo to the harness.

"Go take a look," I told her, nodding toward the mirror on the back of her door.

Lark approached the mirror and turned to the side to study herself. I lay back on the bed and started touching myself as I watched her.

"Is it strange that I like it?" she said, reaching down and touching the dildo.

"Not at all," I said.

Lark turned to me and I could see the desire in her.

"Ready to give it a try?" I asked.

She nodded.

"Then get over here," I said. "Are you okay if I refer to it as your dick?"

I rose onto my knees and moved over to the edge of the bed where she stood.

Lark bit her lip and nodded.

"Lovely. Then may I suck your dick?"

Her eyes closed and she let out a little whimper. "Fuck yes you can."

Now I didn't necessarily get off on the taste of silicone, but that didn't matter. It was the act. I made sure to keep eye contact with Lark as she looked down at me as I treated the dildo as an extension of her body.

"You ready to fuck me, love?" I asked.

"Yes," she said.

I lay back on the bed and grabbed a bottle of lube, squirting just a little bit in my hand before covering the dildo. I was already drenched in anticipation, but I liked adding a little extra smoothness.

Lark took a little bit to position herself at my entrance, teasing me with the dildo.

"Now who's being mean?" I asked as she entered me with the very tip before pulling out.

"This is my first time doing this. I want to get the full experience," she said, pushing inside an inch before leaving again.

"Fuck," I said, grabbing onto her hips as if I could control what she was doing.

"Look at me," Lark said, a little bit of command in her voice. There was a burgeoning top inside her, and I loved those little moments when that side of her came out.

I gazed into her eyes as she pushed halfway into me, and then out.

"Fuck me," I begged.

"Like this?" she said, going halfway again, a little smirk on her face.

"You know what I want," I said.

"What do you want, Syd?" she said.

"I want you to fucking fuck me hard, Lark," I said, growing impatient.

She laughed in her throat.

"Like this?"

She punctuated her words with a hard thrust all the way inside me and I almost cried in relief.

"Yes," I said as she withdrew and slammed into me again. "Exactly like that."

As if she'd been waiting for me to say the word, Lark pounded into me with so much enthusiasm, I was hurtling over the edge of a sharp, hard climax within a short time. I did my best to keep my eyes open as I came, locking my gaze on her. She was so fucking beautiful and powerful and sexy and everything I could ever have possibly wanted that my orgasm lengthened until everything inside me collapsed against the mattress.

When I didn't say anything for a few moments, Lark leaned down to peer into my face.

"Are you alive?" she asked.

I pushed my eyelids open. "Barely."

Lark chuckled and lay next to me. "You liked that," she said, pushing my hair out of my face.

"Hell yeah I did," I said, turning my head so I could continue to look at her. "Did you like it?"

She lifted her top leg. "Why don't you find out?"

The harness was crotchless, so I snuck my hand under the dildo and stroked her entrance, which was dripping.

"I guess you did," I said, plunging two fingers inside her as her eyes fluttered closed and she pushed against me.

It took a little maneuvering, but I was dexterous enough to get her to come with just a few thrusts of my fingers and a few circles of her clit.

Lark flopped onto my chest, pillowing her head on one of my breasts.

"Thanks for letting me borrow your dick," she said.

"It can be yours now. I've never used that one before," I said.

"No one's ever given me a dick before," she said.

"I'm happy to be the first one," I said. "I've got other ones you can try, and if you decide you want to buy your own, you can ask Ezra. Her reviews are really solid."

"Do you have one of those double ended ones?" she asked.

"Maybe," I said.

Lark sat up. "Can we try it?"

"Give me a few more minutes to rest and I'll go grab it," I said, laughing at her enthusiasm. I may have created a sex monster.

"DO you want to sleep in your bed tonight?" she asked after we'd showered.

I shook my head. "Nope. I like yours."

"Okay," she said as we crawled under her covers together and held each other.

There seemed to be something left unsaid, so I turned to face her.

"What is it?" I asked.

She opened her mouth and then changed her mind and kissed me. "Nothing. I'm just tired."

"You sure?" I asked.

"Let's go to bed," she said, getting up to turn off the light.

"JOY, THIS IS EVERLY," I said the next day when Joy happened to "stop by" so she could "buy a present" for someone.

Everly looked a little scared, but Joy smiled at her and shook her hand.

"It's so nice to meet you, Everly," Joy said. "Syd has said nothing but good things about you."

Everly nodded her head, her face red.

Joy wasn't deterred. She pulled Everly aside as a few customers walked in and I went to greet them. By the time I had rung up the sale of two mugs, Joy had Everly laughing at something.

"Absolutely no pressure at all to come, but we'd love to have you. It's in two weeks and we're doing a Valentine's theme since it's near the holiday," Joy said.

"I'll think about it," Everly said. "If I'm not busy."

Joy beamed. "Fantastic. There will be tons of food and drinks, if that helps sway you."

Everly laughed. "I do love both food and drinks."

"I had the feeling you might," Joy said. "Come by the bookstore anytime and I'll give you some free books to welcome you to Arrowbridge."

"Oh, you don't need to do that, I can pay for books," Everly said, but Joy waved her off.

"It's a gift for a new resident," Joy said, and then she had to get back to work.

"She's very kind," Everly said after Joy had left.

"I know. She keeps trying to help me be a better person." I pretended to shudder and Everly laughed.

"From what I've seen, you're a pretty good person," she said.

"Oh no, that's not good. I need to disabuse you of that immediately," I said.

Everly just kept laughing as she went to the back to pack some more orders.

"VALENTINE'S DAY IS COMING UP," Lark said that night as we sat down to dinner on the couch. She'd made one of Layne's easy sheet-pan recipes of chili lime salmon with veggies and rice, and I couldn't get enough, so I had to pause in the act of shoveling food into my face.

"It is," I said, not sure where this was going. I set my fork down and studied her. Lark just kept eating, but the vibe in the room had changed.

She didn't elaborate.

"Is there a reason you brought it up?" I asked.

"Not really, I was just thinking about it," she said, shrugging one shoulder.

"Oh, okay," I said. Why bring it up if she was just thinking about it, though? Perplexing.

"Did you want to do something?" I asked. Was Lark assuming that we'd do that holiday as a couple, even though we were just doing a casual thing?

"Oh, no." She shook her head. "That's really a couple's holiday and we're not."

No, we weren't. We'd agreed that we weren't. I was still confused.

"Did you want to do something?" I asked.

"I mean, no. Since we're not a couple, that would be weird," she said.

"Right," I agreed. "Sooooo we're not doing something for Valentine's Day." I just wanted to confirm with her.

"Because we're not a couple," she said.

"Okay," I said.

Lark didn't say anything else until after we'd finished dinner, put away the leftovers, and had loaded the dishwasher.

"I'm going to read in my room. I'm really tired tonight," she said, pulling away from me when I leaned in to kiss her.

"Everything okay?" I asked.

"Yup," she said, not meeting my eyes.

Obviously, everything wasn't okay, and she had decided to be passive-aggressive instead of talking to me.

"You sure?" I asked one more time.

"Uh huh," she said, heading toward her room.

"Okay," I said, letting her go.

If she were Joy, I would have sat her down on the couch and made her talk this out. Normally I had no qualms about confronting people and getting all our shit out in the open.

It was different with Lark. If she wasn't going to talk to me and wanted to just be a weirdo, then whatever. She could go ahead and do that. Come find me when you're done.

Annoyed, I went to my room and grabbed a stack of books. At least I had the couch to myself. Clementine hopped up to join me and meowed in my face before getting down and running to Lark's door.

"What is it?" I asked. I just wanted to read in peace.

Clem ran back and did the little routine a few times before

I got up and gave him some food, which shut him up for a little while.

"Ridiculous creature," I told him before walking back to the couch.

~

LARK STAYED in her room for the rest of the night, only coming out to get some snacks and to use the bathroom. She pretended to ignore me, and I did the same, only looking up from my book when her back was turned toward me.

Guess we weren't fucking tonight. Didn't matter to me. I had a fleet of vibrators and two hands. I didn't need sex with Lark every single freaking day.

"I'm going to shower," she announced.

"Fine," I said, not looking up from my book. She didn't say anything else and a few moments later I heard the water turn on.

I sighed and tried to read my book, but the words weren't making any sense. All I could think about was Lark naked in the shower, washing her incredible body. Was she touching herself? Was she thinking about me?

I shut the book and got up from the couch, inching toward the door.

After a few seconds, there was an unmistakable sound of a muffled moan and without thinking it through, I opened the door.

"Hey!" Lark said. "I'm in here."

"I know," I said, pulling my clothes off. "I need to shower too."

I waited a second for her to tell me to get the fuck out, but she didn't, so I pulled the shower curtain aside and got in with her.

"What are you doing?" she asked, holding her washcloth in

front of herself, as if it covered anything.

"You've been ignoring me for hours," I said.

"So have you," she said as the water ran down her body.

"Why are you ignoring me?" I asked. "Did I do something?"

She studied me for a few seconds and then reached for me.

"Come here," she said, not answering my question.

Lark pulled me into her arms and under the warm spray. Both of us loved to take extremely hot showers.

Lark kissed me and dropped the washcloth, rubbing her heated body up against mine.

"Are you mad at me?" I asked.

"No," she said, kissing me again. "Please just fuck me, Syd."

I did as the lady asked.

I CHANGED into my pajamas and went to her room to sleep with her, and she didn't try and stop me or tell me to go back to my own room, so I got into bed and held her like usual, but she kept readjusting.

"You good?" I asked after a few minutes of wiggling.

"Yeah," she said, ceasing movement. Lark lay still with me and then she started moving again.

"Okay, do you want the bed to yourself, or is there something wrong?" I asked.

"I'm fine," she said through clenched teeth.

"I think I'm going to sleep in my own bed," I said, letting go of her.

"You don't have to," she said, but she wasn't protesting that hard.

"Goodnight, Lark," I said before shutting her door and going to sleep in my own bed alone.

Chapter Fourteen

SINCE I SLEPT LIKE SHIT, I almost wished I would have gone back and crawled into bed with Lark. I considered it at least a dozen times.

That morning I was a grumpy bitch and Lark didn't seem to want to talk to me anymore.

I didn't know what to do. I'd tried to talk to her and ask what was wrong, but she'd told me she was fine, so short of tying her to the couch (hot), I wasn't sure what else I should do. Hopefully she'd go to work and talk to Mia and come home and be her regular self again. I bet whatever she was mad about didn't even have anything to do with me. I wasn't her whole world, she had lots of other shit going on.

Still, I was annoyed about it all day and even snapped at Everly for the first time.

"Shit, I'm sorry," I said. "I'm not mad at you, I promise. My roommate is being weird, and I think it's affecting me for some reason." I'd never told Everly about the whole thing with Lark, mostly because I barely knew her, and she didn't need to know a ton of personal information about me.

"Have you tried talking to her?" she asked.

"Oh yeah. She keeps saying she's fine, so I stopped bothering and just left her alone," I said.

"Maybe reach out today and see if she wants to sit down and have a talk. Let her know that you're there for her," Everly said.

I guess I could do that. If Lark was Joy, I already would have done that. So why was I treating Lark differently than I would a regular roommate?

"That's smart. I'll do that."

"You could also bring her a treat or something," Everly said as we loaded up the cart with boxes for shipping.

That was an even better idea. Now I just had to figure out what to get her.

"I know I say this at least twenty times a day, but I'm really glad I hired you," I said.

"It's okay, I like hearing it," she said.

WHILE EVERLY WAS at the post office, I thought about what I could bring Lark to get her to open up. Something small, but something meaningful. I also didn't have a lot of shopping options in Arrowbridge if I didn't want to travel or order something online.

She definitely didn't need anything from the pottery store, so that was out. My mind went to food or drinks, since those were easier to get, and then I remembered that time we'd done shots with the pineapple tequila. If that wouldn't get her to talk, then I didn't know what would.

That night when she got home from work, I already had the shot glasses ready.

"What is this?" she asked as I handed her a full shot glass as she set her stuff down and took off her boots.

"Tequila shots," I said, throwing mine back. She gave me a look before drinking her own and handing me the glass.

"Is this some sort of new tradition I'm unaware of?" she asked.

"Something is going on with you and I thought I'd get you drunk enough to talk about it," I said. I might have already had one shot while I was waiting for her.

"Huh," Lark said. "I can't really argue with that logic."

"Want another one?" I asked.

"Yes," she said.

After Lark had her second shot, I dragged her over to the couch and made her sit down.

I took both of her hands in mine and looked into her blue eyes.

"You can talk to me about anything, Lark. I just wanted you to know that," I said.

Lark gazed back at me and swallowed, looking down at our joined hands.

"I can't talk to you about this," she said.

"Why not?" I asked.

"Because... Because..." she stood up and started pacing a little bit. "I need another shot."

She went to the kitchen and downed her third and I waited for her to come back.

"Listen," she said, still pacing. If that was what she needed to do to get this out, then she could go ahead and pace if she had to.

"I agreed to this whole thing between us, the just having sex and still being regular roommates thing with no feelings or commitments or definitions and I was fine with it at first because I knew you didn't do relationships. I figured if that was the only way I could have you, then it was worth it." She stopped pacing and looked at me with tears in her eyes.

"I told myself not to fall for you and that I could put bubble wrap around my heart or just not have feelings for you and that didn't fucking work. Of course it didn't fucking work. I'm so mad at you, Sydney," she said. Her words were kind of jumbled, so it took me a second to tease out where she was going with this.

"What did I do?" I asked slowly, so terrified of the answer.

"You made me fall in love with you. Asshole."

I didn't think the last word was necessary, but that wasn't the most important part of what she said.

"I'm sorry, can you repeat that?" I said, my body starting to shake uncontrollably.

"I said I love you, and I know that's not what you wanted. It's not what I wanted, but it happened and now I'm going to have to move in with my sister and listen to her having loud sex with her fiancée all the time." Tears welled up and spilled down her cheeks and, even more than her words, that affected me so much that I got up from the couch and hugged her.

"Shhh, it's okay," I said as she cried on my shoulder.

What the actual fuck was I supposed to do here? She absolutely was not in love with me, that was for sure. She couldn't be.

"It's not okay," Lark said, and I pulled back and wiped her eyes with my sleeves.

"This is not a big deal, Lark," I said.

"Me being in love with you isn't a big deal?" she asked.

"No, because you're not in love with me," I said gently.

Lark's eyes narrowed and she pushed me away. I almost fell against the coffee table, but I caught myself at the last second.

"Fuck you, Sydney," she said, pointing at me with a shaking finger. "How dare you? How fucking *dare* you?!"

"What?!" I said, completely taken aback at her intense reaction. "Why are you mad?"

Lark closed her eyes and took a deep breath through her nose, as if she was gathering her thoughts.

"I just told you that I loved you, and you decided that apparently I don't know what I'm talking about. I guess I don't know my own feelings," she said, her voice dripping in sarcasm. "You have got some seriously fucked up ideas about how emotions work, Sydney. You've just decided to exempt yourself from falling in love, as if that's a thing that you can just do. A switch you can turn on or turn off. And I did try! But I love you anyway and right now, I really wish I didn't."

Her words were like physical blows. Like slices from a knife. She was angry and she was hurt, and it was all directed at me.

"I'm sorry," I said automatically.

"Fuck you," she said, before turning and going to her room, slamming the door so loud that the neighbors were going to complain.

I got up and poured myself another shot.

After Lark went to her room, I sat on the couch and tried to figure out what the hell had just happened.

Lark said she was in love with me. Everything came down to that. When had it happened? If she was feeling that way, she should have told me sooner. I would have stopped fucking her, that was for sure. I'd have put the brakes on everything we'd been doing. Seeing her hurting was awful. It made me sick.

She deserved someone who could love her back. Lark deserved to be fucking cherished like the treasure she was. She deserved fireworks and vacations to private islands and chocolates and diamonds and all that shit.

I couldn't give her what she needed. I couldn't love her in the way she deserved. It wasn't my path. I'd thought we'd been going in the same direction and now I didn't have a map for where to go next.

Apologizing and seeing if she was okay seemed to be the first step, so I made up a little snack plate and grabbed a glass of water and knocked on her door.

"Lark?" I asked.

"Fuck off," she said.

"I brought you something to eat. I can make you some dinner if you want," I said.

"What part of 'fuck off' don't you understand?" she said.

"It's just that… I'd leave this out here, but I don't want Clementine to eat it," I said.

Lark cursed a bunch of times before she opened the door.

"What?" she snapped.

"Snacks?" I said, holding the plate up.

"Are you serious right now?" she asked.

"Yes?" I said.

Lark's eyes narrowed. "I am still incredibly pissed off at you, but I'm also hungry."

I waved the plate under her nose. "Can I come in and talk?"

Her eyes were red from crying and I just wanted to throw the plate and hug her.

"I guess," she said, snatching the plate from me. I pushed the door open and sat on the edge of her bed.

"Hydration," I said, handing the water to her. She drained the glass and set it down on her nightstand.

Lark nibbled at the snacks and I waited for her to say something.

"You don't have anything to say?" she asked.

"About…" I said, trailing off.

"I have never fantasized about strangling someone before this moment," she said, closing her eyes.

"I mean, you can choke me if you want," I said. That would be so sexy.

"Sydney. If I have to tell you to be serious one more time, I'm going to throw you out the window," Lark said.

"I'm sorry," I said automatically. "I am."

"I told you I love you and your only reaction was to tell me that I couldn't possibly love you, and then you brought me snacks," she said.

"Yes?" I said.

"Can you do me just one tiny favor?" she asked.

"Of course," I said.

Lark pushed the plate aside and crawled over to me, straddling my lap and looking down at me.

"What's the favor?" I asked, almost completely breathless.

"Kiss me," she said, running her fingers through my curls. "Kiss me and tell me what you feel."

That was no hardship.

I grabbed her ass and pulled her closer and tilted my head up as her mouth met mine, fiery and forceful. This kiss was making a point and I followed her lead, moaning as she seduced me with lips and tongue and her fingers in my hair and on the back of my neck.

She was so sexy and wonderful and sweet and delicious, and I couldn't imagine ever wanting to kiss anyone else but her.

Whoa. Hold on.

What was *that*?

Lark felt me freeze and pulled back.

"Everything okay?" she asked, and I couldn't look away from her face. Her beautiful, lovely face.

I opened my mouth and then shut it and shook my head.

"Syd?" she asked.

"Kiss me again," I said. "I need to check something."

She did so immediately and all of the things I'd been thinking rushed to my mind again and my entire body was suffused by a warm certainty that wrapped around me.

"I love you," I tried to say, but her tongue was still in my mouth, so it just came out as gibberish.

She pulled back again. "What?"

"I love you?" I said, testing the words again.

Lark's eyes narrowed. "Is that a question or a statement?"

I tried again. "I love you." And again. "I love you." I tried emphasizing a different word each time. "*I* love you. I *love* you. I love *you*."

"Syd? Are you broken?" she asked, brushing my hair back and looking a little worried.

"No," I said. "I'm not broken."

And I wasn't. I'd always thought love would be awful. It would mean giving up myself to someone else. It would mean that I'd have to change my entire life and become a different person. That I would be miserable. Nothing about this was miserable. This woman in my arms was everything.

She did deserve better than me, that was for damn sure, but I was also too selfish to give her up. Guess I was enough of an asshole for that.

"I love you," I said again, purely for the joy of saying it, and then I started laughing and couldn't stop.

"What's so funny?"

Lark was probably questioning her love for me right now, but I didn't care.

"I thought love would be terrible," I said. "But it's actually good."

Lark stared down at me. "Why did you think love was going to be terrible?"

"Because it ruins so many people, I don't know. It was something I didn't think I needed. I was fine on my own. I was fine doing my life without it. Then I met you and now I can't think of doing life without you by my side, and it's not just because of the sex, even though that's incredible. I like making dinner with you and sitting on the couch and making burrito jokes and everything. I loved taking care of you when you were sick and drunk. I love having the most random conversations about absolutely nothing with you. Everything with you is better, Lark."

There were tears in her eyes again, but I hoped they were happy tears this time.

"For someone who didn't want to fall in love, you're awfully good at romantic speeches," she said, sniffing. I offered her my sleeve to wipe her nose. I could have gotten her a tissue, but I didn't want her to move. She needed to stay right where she was.

"That was my first one. I'm glad to know you liked it. I didn't write a script or anything," I said. "Watching all those movies and reading all those romance books must have paid off." I ran my hands up and down her back, gradually sneaking them under her shirt so I could feel her skin.

"My romantic burrito," she said, laughing a little and kissing my forehead.

"Your romantic burrito," I said.

"Mmmm mmm mmmmmmm," she said as she kissed me again.

TURNED out that declarations of love could lead to absolutely mind-blowing sex. I might have considered making one sooner if I'd known that part. Maybe.

During a break, Lark and I lay together and she asked me about some of my past partners. I was surprised she wanted to know, but she said she was curious.

"I mean, none of that matters because now I have you. I'm a one-woman woman now. You can watch me delete all my apps," I said. Honestly, doing that would be kind of a relief. No more wondering if I was going to end up with someone who was compatible, or if I would have to send a 911 message to Joy so she could call me with an "emergency" to give me a reason to leave.

"Who was your first?" I asked her. We'd spent a lot of time

talking about me and I realized I'd never really asked her about her past relationships.

Lark dived under the blankets, pulling them up over her head.

"Lark?" I asked, pulling them down, fighting with her grip. "What is it? Did you have sex with someone embarrassing? Come on, you can tell me. I won't judge."

There was no way she had had more shameful sex than I had.

Lark's face finally popped back out from under the blanket.

"Who was it?" I asked. "Is it someone I know?"

She nodded.

"Oh my god, who?"

Lark took a breath. "You."

"Me?" I said. "That doesn't make sense."

"You were my first," she said. "I'd never had sex with anyone else before you."

I stared at her in shock. "So that night at the bar?"

"Yup," she said.

"That was your first time with a partner?" I asked.

She nodded, her face red.

"Holy shit, this is blowing my mind," I said. "You've only been with me?"

"Only you," she said. "I'm sorry I didn't tell you. At first I didn't want to, and then I figured we'd been together so many times that it didn't matter anymore. Are you upset?"

I shook my head. "No, I just wish that you would have told me. I might have done things differently if I'd known."

"I'm sorry I didn't tell you," she said. "But I think we figured it out."

I rolled her until she was under me.

"For someone without a lot of experience, you definitely learned pretty fast," I said, pushing my hips against hers.

She moaned. "I had a good teacher."

"Ohhh, I like the idea of being your sex teacher. That's hot."

Lark let out a sound that was halfway between a gasp and a giggle.

"What's my grade?" she said.

"Oh, I don't know, I'm going to have to give you another test," I said at the same time as I stroked her core with my hand.

"I'll pass," she said, her eyes fluttering closed.

"We'll see about that," I said, kissing my way down her body.

Chapter Fifteen

"Good morning, love," I said when Lark's eyes opened the next day when her alarm went off.

"I like it when you call me that," she said softly. "I'm only a little bit hung over."

"Same," I said. There was a ghost of a headache knocking on my skull, so I got up and grabbed some aspirin and water for both of us.

"Thanks, babe," she said.

"Babe?" I asked.

"Yeah, I'm trying it out. You like?"

I usually reserved that word for my friends, but I couldn't lie, I loved hearing it from Lark's lips. To be fair, she could have called me "Bitchslut" and I would have viewed it as a term of endearment.

"I like it when you call me Syd," I said, gathering her in my arms and wrapping my legs around her too. I did not want to get up and go to work today.

"I'll alternate," she said, burrowing into my neck.

"Hey," I said, and her head lifted.

"What?" she said.

"How about you call out of work today? Play hooky with me." Everly was still new, but she was more than up to the task of managing the shop today, along with Mom.

"I did miss time when I was sick, how about a half day? I can pretend I have some sort of appointment," she said.

"I'll take what I can get," I said as I sent a message to my mom and Everly that I would be in that afternoon and to let me know if there was some kind of emergency. Mom was surprised, since I almost never took any time off. Everly was sweet, telling me that if I needed the whole day, that she could handle things.

Lark had also been on her phone letting Liam know that she'd be in later. After a few back and forth messages, she tossed her phone on her nightstand.

"Free?" I asked.

"Free for you," she said.

Fuck, I loved her.

LARK AND I engaged in some slow morning sex before making breakfast together and eating it in bed.

"Are we dating now?" I asked, sliding the last bite of fried potatoes over to her. This relationship had really changed me already. I didn't normally share food with many people.

"Yes? I think that's the general idea," Lark said.

"I don't know, I've never done this part before. I'm new," I said.

Lark snorted. "It's so weird that you're so experienced with sex, but not dating. For most people it's the reverse."

"Well, I'm unique," I said, tossing my hair.

"That's why I like you," she said, setting the tray aside.

I turned on my side so I could stare at her. "I thought you *loved* me."

She rolled her eyes. "Yes, I love you, but I like you too. They don't always go together."

"I guess that's true. Well, I like you and I love you. So there."

Lark pulled the covers over our heads, her eyes sparkling in the dark.

"Did you ever read books under the covers with a light so your mom didn't know you were staying up late?" she asked.

"Yeah," I said. "Even though she probably wouldn't have done anything or punished me. It was more fun to be sneaky about it."

"My mother definitely would have been pissed. She didn't want me reading so much," Lark said.

"I know I've said this before, but I really don't like your mother. At all."

"That's fine, I don't like her either."

I told Lark more about what it had been like with my mom, how she did her best, and I would step up and handle what I could.

"You're like Honor that way. She was more of a parent to me in the sense that she taught me how to ride a bike and pick out my clothes and make breakfast and that kind of thing. She wasn't even that much older herself, but Honor has always been mature since day one."

It was impossible for me to picture Honor as a child. I'd love to see some pictures to prove that it had even happened.

"Do you, um, do you think about kids?" Lark asked, picking at something on her sheets.

"You mean having kids?" I asked.

She nodded. "I know everything is so new with us, but I think we should talk about the important stuff and not put it off."

"Shit, Lark. That's a lot to think about. I'm just getting used to the idea of a committed relationship. Can I have some time to think about it?" I asked. The air under the blanket was starting to get a little too warm.

"Yeah, definitely," she said. "Sorry. We don't have to talk about it right now. Let's go back to talking about books."

She did change the subject back to books, but now that she'd planted the idea of kids in my brain, I couldn't stop turning it over.

One thing I knew without a doubt: my future included Lark. I'd never fantasized about marriage or babies or any of that because it had always seemed like something for someone else. But marriage with Lark? Seeing her in a white dress and sliding a ring on her finger didn't seem so bad. And then I imagined what she'd look like pregnant, her belly round. A sweet little baby with blonde hair and blue eyes. I'd take care of her when her ankles were swollen. When the baby was born, I'd be on bottle duty at night so she could sleep.

All of those things suddenly didn't seem so scary or strange.

"What are you thinking about?" Lark asked when I'd been silent for a little while.

"Our future," I said. "Whenever my friends would talk about futures, mine always seemed so blurry. And then I met you and things got a whole lot clearer. I don't know, I guess I can just see a lot of different possibilities now."

She smiled and kissed me.

"As long as we're doing it together, the rest will fall into place," she said. The certainty in her voice made my heart want to explode.

"I like the way that sounds," I said.

LARK AND I went off to work and I ended up sending a message in my group chat with Layne and Joy that Lark and I were officially together. I didn't mention the first hookup. That was going to be my little sexy secret with Lark.

I knew it I knew it Joy pay up Layne sent.

Hold on, did you make a bet on me? I responded.

Maybe Joy sent.

We bet if you would get your head out of your ass before Valentine's Day or after Layne sent. **I voted for before so now I win.**

Congrats? I sent. **What did you win?**

Pizza from Nick's Layne sent. **With drinks and sides and dessert.**

They were ridiculous.

"Thanks for covering for me this morning," I said to Everly, putting my phone aside.

"No problem. It was a little scary at first, but nothing got broken or stolen and I even made five sales," she said, and I could tell she was proud of herself.

"Good job. I should leave you in charge more often."

Her face went pale. "Maybe not until next week."

I laughed. "Don't worry, I'll be here."

"ARE we doing anything for Valentine's Day now?" I asked Lark that night as we put dinner together. "We never really resolved that."

"Oh, I don't know. If you wanted to do something."

We had book club the night before, but Valentine's Day was on Friday, so we could do something that night.

"I could order dinner and you could pick it up on your way home."

Her eyes lit up. Oh, she liked that idea.

"Yes, please," she said. Lark might not be as fancy as Honor, but she did enjoy finer things.

"And gifts? Should we set a price limit?" I asked.

"How about fifty bucks?' she said.

"Perfect," I agreed.

"You know," she said, slicing a radish thinly, "for someone who's never had a relationship, you've gotten pretty good at it so far."

"Thanks." I smiled and leaned over to kiss her mouth. "I'm definitely going to fuck up at some point, so I'd lower your expectations."

Lark snorted. "I think you're better than you think you are. I'm choosing to be optimistic."

"You have to think I'm better because you *love* me."

Lark tilted her head to the side with a smile. "You really like that, don't you?"

"I always thought it would be terrible, but I fucking love it. I love that you love me," I said, taking her knife from her grip and setting it down so I could hold her. "I can't get enough of it. Now I understand why people are always writing songs and shit."

I swayed us from side to side, even though there was no music playing in the apartment.

"You gonna write me a song?" Lark asked.

"Absolutely not. I have no musical talent. But how about if I let you sit on my face?"

Lark burst out laughing. "That's just as good."

Chapter Sixteen

"HELP. I don't know what to get Lark for Valentine's Day," I said to Layne and Joy as we had dinner together at Joy's a few nights later. Ezra had a writing deadline and had actually rented a hotel room for the night to get everything done. Lark had gone to Mia's to hang out. It was the first time we'd separated from each other, aside from when we went to work, and I was already missing her like we'd been apart for months.

Eating at Joy and Ezra's was always interesting due to the sex toys that were on display in the living room, as if they were just those creepy little angel figurines that grandmothers collected. I was all for taking away the shame around sex toys and all that, but it was hard to eat my dinner when there was a neon dragon cock right in my line of sight.

"You know that it's on Friday, right?" Joy said. "You've got to get your shit together."

"I know, I know. I just...nothing seems right," I said. I'd already shot down dozens of ideas.

"It should be something special and unique," Layne said.

"Yes, exactly. But what? She's apparently making me something and I know it's going to be amazing and better than anything I could do." Not for the first time, I wished I had any talent with pottery. Making her a custom mug or a bowl or something would have been right from the heart and just for her, but alas. I didn't have the skills.

"What if you didn't make it, but you commissioned it?" Joy asked. "You know Kendra's friend, Hollis? She just asked her to make some custom romance cover posters for the shop. What about something like that?"

"Oh, like those vintage covers with a woman swooning and her boobs spilling out of her dress kind of thing?" I asked.

"Yeah. Have her do one of you and Lark together and blow it up."

The idea of that made me laugh and it would be unique.

"Reach out to Kendra and have her put you in touch with Hollis. I bet she'd give you a good rate," Joy said.

"Thanks, I think I will, even if it's just a backup idea. Right now, the best idea I have is orgasm coupons," I said.

Both Layne and Joy burst out laughing.

"Maybe that's your last resort present," Layne said.

"What are you getting for Honor?" I asked.

"Well, we agreed since we got engaged that we're not doing gifts this year, but I bought an extra bottle of her favorite perfume during a Black Friday sale that I've been saving. And I'm going to kidnap her and take her out for a fancy dinner. She's going to be so mad." Layne was giggling with glee at this prospect.

"Ezra and I aren't technically buying anything, so we're each giving each other a fantasy night." Joy's face got red. "I'll let you use your imagination as to what that would entail."

For someone dating a future sex therapist, Joy could be pretty close-mouthed about her own sex life.

"I feel like every night is already fantasy night, so that's out." I sighed and grabbed another biscuit to cover with the whipped honey butter that Layne had made.

"You look happy though," Joy said, putting her hand on my arm. "I love seeing it."

"Thanks," I said. "I am happy. It's the worst."

They both laughed.

"I know what you mean," Layne said. "Sometimes I'm just so overcome with love for Honor that I feel like I need to scream or punch a wall or something."

I nodded. "Sometimes Lark is so cute, I forget how to breathe."

"Awww," Layne and Joy said at the same time.

"Shut the fuck up," I said, pointing at both of them with my fork.

"Sydney's in looovvvvveeeee," Joy sang.

I covered my ears. "Shut upppppppp."

~

I SENT an email to Hollis the next day after looking her up online and she got back to me right away and seemed enthusiastic about my request.

I'd be happy to help you out! I'd just need some headshots of both of you that I can blend into the stock images I already have, if you didn't want to do a photoshoot and keep it as a surprise.

That might be a little tricky, but I went through my phone and I had more than a few pictures of Lark that I'd taken that I hoped would work. I sent them and some of myself, along with a few ideas and Hollis said she'd get to work right away. Her rates were so reasonable that I told her I could pay a rush fee, since I needed to get the damn thing ordered and overnight shipped so I could give it to Lark on Friday. I hoped she wouldn't hate it.

Everly thought it was a great idea, but I signed her paycheck, so she might have just been trying to be nice to me.

"Do you have a Valentine this year?" I asked.

She shook her head. "No, it will just be me, but my moms are going on a weekend trip together so I'll have the house to myself." At last Everly had opened up about her life a little. Her moms had had her when they were older, so they'd both just recently retired and bought a house in Arrowbridge. Everly had moved in with them when her last lease had ended and was trying to get on her feet. Reading between the lines, she'd been handed a few challenges and had needed a soft place to land and her moms to help pick her back up.

"You should do all the things you want to do. Be your own Valentine. Have a date with yourself," I said.

"I like that idea. I love my moms, but they're a little over-bearing most of the time and I think they still have a hard time realizing I'm a fully grown adult and don't need to be super-vised." She spoke of them with nothing but affection, but I bet that was stifling.

"You should talk to Joy about that. She used to have so much drama with her mom." Drama was an understatement.

"Maybe," Everly said. "Let me get through book club first."

HOLLIS SENT me the first draft of the image she'd put together the next day. I almost fell off my chair when I looked at it during work. The image was of me, wearing a beautiful dark blue gown, holding Lark as she swooned, her hair blowing behind her as if by a breeze. We were in front of a castle. Of course.

When Hollis had asked for a title for the book, I'd joked and said Only One Burrito and then I hadn't been able to come up with anything else, so she'd kept it in swirling font, and then added a little burrito in Lark's hand.

It was so ridiculous and so sexy at the same time, and I

hoped Lark was going to love it. Hollis sent me the image and I placed the order for a poster and a frame with overnight shipping.

That night I was trying to figure out what to do for dinner when Lark walked in looking very smug.

"Did you have a good day, love?" I asked. I couldn't get enough of calling her that.

"I did," she said, kissing me softly. "What are you making?"

"I don't know. One of us needs to be more organized about this. Joy used to make lists and meal plans," I said.

"I can do that," Lark said. "I mean, if you're okay with that."

"Go for it. I know I'm not going to get my act together enough to keep it up every week," I said.

"Okay. I'll make a grocery list this weekend and we can sit down and plan."

"That sounds like something a couple would do," I said. "Go for romantic walks in the frozen food aisle."

Lark gasped as if this just occurred to her. "Good thing we are a couple."

"Oh yeah, we are," I said, pulling her in for another kiss. "Now help me take some of these ingredients and make some actual food."

"I will, but only because I love you," she said, and I squeezed her ass.

EVERLY SEEMED to be on edge all of Thursday and I told her that she didn't have to go to book club if she was stressing out about it.

"I know it's not a big deal," she said. "I, um, I have a little bit of anxiety around new people."

That was obvious, but I didn't say that.

"You can always bail if you need to and no one will judge you. I'll show you where the back entrance is, and it's near the bathroom, so you can just pretend you have to pee and escape out the back."

Everly sighed in gratitude. "Thanks. I know it's embarrassing, but it's just kind of how my brain works."

"Brains can be mean sometimes," I said. "If you ever need any kind of accommodations to make your job easier, please let me know."

She blinked at me a few times and then turned her face away, as if to hide a few tears from me. It wasn't that big of a deal, but she seemed like she'd been treated badly in the past by someone, or by a lot of someones.

"That means a lot," she said, and I busied myself arranging mugs so she didn't feel like I was staring at her.

"You're welcome," I said.

Everly cleared her throat and then said she was going to dust some of the shelves.

THURSDAY EVENING, I closed the shop, told Everly I'd see her in a few hours at book club, went upstairs to change my clothes, decompress, and then headed back down to Mainely Books to help Joy out with setting up.

"It looks like Hallmark threw up in here," I said as I walked by a pile of heart-shaped lights, exploding heart centerpieces, and a stack of plastic hearts that needed to be hung from the hooks on the ceiling that Kendra's girlfriend Theo had installed to make decorating a whole lot easier. Ezra was pulling out the ladder and I assumed she'd be the one climbing it while Joy directed.

"What do you need?" I asked Joy, who was frazzled, as usual.

"Food table, place those decorations, drinks, you know the drill," she said, starting to untangle the heart lights.

"Got it," I said. I'd just covered the food table with a red shiny tablecloth when Lark came in.

"Hey," she said, giving me a kiss. "Need help?"

"Always," I said, taking pleasure in seeing her face for the first time since this morning. "Fuck, you're so pretty."

She blushed and giggled, which made her even prettier. Fuck.

"You've gotta stop looking at me like that or else I'm going to have to drag you upstairs," she said in my ear.

I stifled a groan. "You have to stop saying things like that to me, because you know that I'm going to picture it."

"That'll just get you ready for later," she whispered, brushing her hand down my side before grabbing a bag of cups.

She was going to be the death of me.

EVERLY DID SHOW up to book club, and I made sure that Lark and I sat with our chairs in the same direction as the back exit. She didn't contribute anything, but she stayed the entire time and even had some snacks at the end before coming over to thank me for inviting her.

"Thanks for coming, and don't forget to vote for the next book when they send out the email tomorrow," I said.

She nodded and headed out.

"I am prettier than her," Lark said after Everly had left.

"Of course you are, love," I said as I cut another piece of cake. This one was a strawberry shortcake and it was to die for.

"She's a nice girl, though," she said. "Seems like she might have a little social anxiety."

I nodded and licked some of the whipped marshmallow frosting off my finger.

"She told me a little bit about it, and I told her where the exits were in case she needed to bail. That's got to be rough."

"If she ever needs a place to have dinner, you can invite her over with us. We're non-threatening," she said.

I gave her a look.

"Well, I am," she amended.

MY GIFT for Lark arrived the next morning and I ran upstairs to get it and put it in the frame. I decided not to wrap it, and instead store it in my room and bring it out with a flourish tonight.

Nick was running a heart-shaped pizza special that Lark was going to pick up for dinner and the only plans I had for this weekend involved Lark and her bed, and as many toys as both of us owned. With occasional breaks for food and showering and sleep.

I may have also done a quick search of the apartment for anything that was present-like but didn't find anything.

It was torture waiting for Lark to get home. I was nearly vibrating out of my skin and ran to the door when I heard someone on the stairs, looking through the peephole to make sure it was Lark. She had the pizza box in her arms with a huge bag on top.

I heard her curse as she realized she couldn't unlock the door, so I opened it for her.

"Let me take that," I said, putting my hands under the pizza box.

"Thanks," she said a little breathlessly. I set the box and bag on the counter and kissed her thoroughly.

"Happy Valentine's Day," I said when I finally broke the kiss. She looked a little dazed.

"Happy Valentine's Day," she said, giving me one more kiss.

"I really, really want my present, but I'm also hungry, so should we have dinner first?" I asked.

"Food, please," she said, putting both hands on her belly.

Clementine screamed as if to agree, even though he had literally just eaten.

"Food for humans," I told him. He just screamed again.

AFTER WE'D STUFFED ourselves with pizza, we sat on the couch and I stared expectantly at Lark.

"Your present isn't wrapped, because I couldn't really wrap it," she said.

"Yours isn't wrapped either, but that's only because I didn't have the time or energy," I said.

"Should I go first?" she asked. Her fingers kept twisting and untwisting together and one of her legs bounced up and down on the floor. Why was she so stressed about a present?

"You seem like you want to go first," I said. If she waited any longer, I thought she might explode.

She inhaled deeply and nodded.

I waited for her to pull something out of her pocket or get up to go get something. Instead, she opened her mouth and started to sing.

Lark had sung various songs for me before, but this one I didn't recognize. It was soft and sort of folky and with her deeper voice it hit me in the center of my chest. Mesmerized, I watched as she performed the song on the couch for me as tears started to fall from my eyes at how incredible she was.

It took until the second time she hit the chorus for me to

realize that the reason that I didn't recognize this song was that she'd written it.

Lark had written me a fucking song.

I felt awful for sniffing during her performance, but I couldn't help it. I was losing it. Lark held the last note and looked at me, her face still dreamy from wherever she went when she performed.

"Holy shit," I said, grabbing some tissues. "I don't even know what to say to that because I don't have the right words. My god, Lark."

I was honestly a little scared of her after that.

"You liked it?" she asked in a small voice.

"I loved it. I beyond loved it. No one's ever written a song for me before. I can't imagine how much work that was, fuck, come here."

I kissed her beautiful mouth and tried to show her how much I appreciated this unbelievable gift. If I hadn't already been completely and totally in love with her, that would have absolutely done it.

"You liked it?" she said, pulling back as I held her face between my hands.

"Yes," I said. "Yes, I did."

Her smile was everything.

"I can't exactly top that, but, well, here you go," I said, feeling like absolute shit about my present as I turned the frame around and showed it to her. Compared to hers, mine was silly and ridiculous. If only I had an ounce of artistic talent. Maybe I should have gone with sex coupons.

Lark's mouth dropped open.

"Oh my god," she said, staring at the picture. "This is us!"

"Yeah, I had a book cover artist make it."

Lark let out a loud laugh. "Oh my god, this is amazing! I love it!"

She stared at the picture for a while, taking it all in.

"There's even a burrito, holy shit. This is the best thing I've ever seen."

"You like it?" I asked.

"I adore it," she said, kissing me and then going back to the poster.

"Now I'm going to want more of these done in different cover styles," she said. "How cute would we be on one of those illustrated covers? Or a really dark moody one?"

"I can ask Hollis if she could make more. She said she loved doing it," I told her.

Lark stood up and glanced around. "Now we just have to figure out where to put it. I'd love to have it in my room, but it doesn't seem right to keep it to myself. How about here?" She pointed to a spot of wall near the TV that had a few random pictures that Joy had bought and hadn't taken with her when she moved. They'd been hung up for so long that I didn't even notice them anymore.

"You think it will work?" she said, going over and holding up the poster.

"We'll make it work," I said, putting my hand on her back.

"Thank you for this, it's perfect," she said, puckering her lips for a kiss.

"It's not, but your song was. Beyond perfect," I said. "Will you sing it for me again?"

"After we hang up my poster," she said.

Chapter Seventeen

"How was your weekend?" Everly asked when she came in on Monday.

"Good," I said through a yawn. Lark and I had turned Valentine's Day into Valentine's weekend and had done exactly what I'd hoped we would, and more. I was tired and sore and so completely in love that it felt like I was floating most of the time.

I'd wake up in the middle of the night in bed with Lark and be so overwhelmed with it that I had to wipe a few tears before I got up to pee. Love was…a lot.

"Did she like the present?" she asked as we waited for customers to walk in.

"She did. Hers was better, though," I said. "She wrote me a song."

Everly's eyes went wide. "Wow. That's amazing."

"I know," I said with a sigh. "She's amazing. I can't even believe that she's mine."

"You look happy," Everly observed.

"Thanks," I said. "I am happy. It's a weird feeling. I always rolled my eyes at my friends when they talked about their partners and now I know exactly what they were talking about. They're so smug about it."

The group chat had been quiet over the weekend, but it had lit up this morning with me gushing about Lark and then my two best friends mocking the shit out of me for everything I'd ever said to them about love.

It might have bothered me if I wasn't so blissed out.

I miss you. Why do I miss you? I saw you this morning and I'm going to see you in a few hours Lark sent as I was heading to lunch with Joy.

I know. I miss you too. Send me a picture of your face, please. I want to stare at it I responded.

"I've become one of those people," I announced to Joy as we got in line to order.

"What people?" she asked.

"The kind of people who are so disgustingly in love, that they annoy others with it." Lark sent me a cute selfie from the coffee shop and I smiled.

"I told you that love was going to hit you hard," Joy said. "But you never listen to me."

"I do listen to you! I listen to you all the time," I said.

Joy smirked at me and we ordered our food and sat down at our table.

"All teasing aside, I have to tell you how proud I am of you," Joy said.

I wanted to make a joke, but her words actually made me emotional. "Thanks, Joy. Although I don't really know what I did. I fell in love with an incredibly hot girl, I didn't cure cancer."

"Letting someone love you isn't easy, and you were very resistant to it."

That was an understatement. I couldn't count how many times I'd said that love just wasn't for me. I was both opposed and allergic to it.

"Lark wore me down," I said. "But it's not like I put up a ton of resistance."

Maybe telling her that we could be roommates who fuck and go back to our regular lives after we'd done it wasn't the best idea. But I was always a fan of bad ideas.

～

"DO you always want to live in Arrowbridge?" Lark asked me later that night as we lounged together after dinner on the couch, feeding each other cookies and watching the lesbian baseball show. It was so mundane, but I was so fucking happy.

"I might like to go be somewhere else for a while. Just to see, you know? I mean, I went away for college, but that doesn't really count. I didn't have a reason to go anywhere else, and now with you and my best friends and my job here, I don't have something taking me anywhere else."

Lark nodded and twisted apart one of the cookies and licked at the cream inside. Fuck. What were we talking about?

"It's not a bad place to live. I feel pretty settled here, but maybe we could go on a trip somewhere. I haven't been on a trip in a long time," she said.

"We can go on a trip." One of the bonuses of Lark moving in had been her picking up half of the rent and utilities and groceries so I was back in the black in my bank account again. With Everly's help, the pottery shop was doing better, and we were finally expanding our online business. If things kept up the way they were headed, I was going to hire Everly on full-time.

Lark chuckled.

"What is it?" I asked.

She turned her face to mine. "I was just thinking about how much me being with you would disappoint my mother."

"Listen, if you ever need to see her, I'm happy to go with

you and completely horrify her with how much money I don't have," I said.

She threw her head back and laughed fully.

"Oh my god, we might have to do that just so I can see her face," Lark said.

I paused the show and crawled into her lap. "I have sooo much credit card debt," I said, licking her neck.

"Mmmmm, tell me more," she gasped.

"I will never pay off my student loans," I said, sucking on that one spot on her neck that drove her wild.

Lark moaned again.

"I have no idea what a 401k is have no plans of learning," I said, pinching her nipple, making her arch into me before I went back to her mouth and then slid my hand into her pants, finding her wet.

"Guess you like hearing about that," I said.

"Mmmmm mmm mmmmm," she said, "tell me more."

"Tax the rich," I said, sliding two fingers into her.

"I don't know why this is working for me," Lark said, letting out a little breathless laugh as I stroked her inside.

"Should I keep going?" I asked.

"*Yes*," she said, so I did.

"IF YOU WANTED to see your mom, I would go with you, you know," I said later as we lounged in the tub together.

"I don't want to now, but maybe someday," she said, swirling her fingers through the scented water.

"That's great too," I said. "You should probably meet my mom in some sort of official capacity, though." Lark had briefly met my mom as my roommate, but she hadn't been introduced as my girlfriend.

"We could make her dinner or something," Lark said. "Bring it over to her."

"That sounds perfect," I said. "She'd love that."

"I love you," she said, and I had to kiss her.

"I love you," I said. "And you know what's a bonus in falling for your roommate?"

"What's that?" she asked.

"I don't have to ask you to move in with me because you already live here," I said. "We get to skip that whole step."

"That's true," she said with a giggle. "Does that mean you're going to move into my room?"

"We can put your bed in mine, if you want, since my room is bigger," I said.

"I like that idea. What if we move all the bookshelves and our clothes into what's my room now?" she asked.

The water had started to cool, so I pulled the plug to let a little bit out so we could prolong our bath.

"So it will be a library slash closet," I said. "That's such a good idea."

Lark beamed. "I think so. And someday we can have a whole room as a library in our house."

"Oh, we have a house now, do we?" I asked.

"Yeah," she said as I turned on the hot water again. "I'd love to have a house with you."

That was another thing I'd pictured. A house with a yard. Not too big, not too small. We could get another cat or two, or maybe a dog and have our friends over for dinner parties like adults.

"I'd love that too," I said. "I can't wait to face the future with you."

"Are you scared?" she asked.

"I'd be lying if I said I wasn't. I'm scared about a lot of things, but now they're different fears. Before meeting you, I thought the scariest thing would be love, and now the scariest thing to me would be losing it. Losing you," I said.

"You're not going to lose me," Lark said. "I'm yours."

She sat up in the tub, sloshing water onto the floor.

"And I'm all yours," I said. "You're stuck with me."

"I couldn't be happier," she said.

"Me neither," I said, kissing her again.

Epilogue

"JOY REALLY WENT ALL OUT," Lark said as we pulled up to Layne and Honor's engagement party two months later.

"Hey, I helped," I said.

"Yes, you did," Lark said, kissing my cheek before we got out of the car and walked toward Mark's house. Joy had thought about renting a space, but it was easier to do it at Mark and Sadie's, not to mention their house was incredible.

"I'm sure my mother is still pissed that my sister didn't manage to make Mark his wife. I never thought she'd do something like fall in love with Mark's nanny, but I'm so glad she did," Lark said.

We went right inside with our gift and the house was filled with people.

Lark and I set our present on the table Joy had marked for the purpose and went to find the happy couple. They were both in the kitchen, of course, along with Mark, Sadie, and a tall woman I didn't recognize.

"Hey, everything looks amazing," I said, hugging both Layne and Honor. "Where's Joy?"

Layne pointed to Joy, who was working the room, with Ezra following behind her with a tray of drinks.

"Congratulations again," Lark said, hugging Honor.

"Thank you, little sister," Honor said.

"This is Mark's niece, Ryan. She came up for the party and she's going to be visiting this summer," Layne said, directing our attention to the new woman. In addition to being tall, she reminded me a little bit of Honor, except Ryan seemed even chillier. From her bleached blonde hair cut short and her ice-blue eyes, she was intimidating to say the least.

"Nice to meet you," she said, shaking my hand with busi-nesslike efficiency.

"Nice to meet you," I repeated, giving Lark a look.

Riley and Zoey, the twins that Layne looked after, ran into the kitchen.

"Can we give you our present now?" they asked in unison. "Please?"

Layne looked at Honor. "What do you think?"

"I say yes," Honor said.

They squealed and ran off to fetch whatever it was.

"Let's go save Joy from herself," I told Lark.

"That's a good idea."

We eventually found Joy, but Ezra had pulled her into a corner and was talking to her and stroking her hair.

"I think Ezra has it handled," I said to Lark.

"Yeah, something tells me they're going to disappear for an unspecified amount of time," Lark said, wiggling her eyebrows.

"Definitely," I agreed and a few seconds later, Ezra took Joy's hand and started pulling her down the hall.

Lark and I said hello to Liam and Gwen, who, according to Lark, were also on their way to an engagement. Mark stood up and made a toast, and then Joy emerged with mussed hair and a dazed expression to make another.

Layne called for everyone's attention and smiled as she looked around at everyone, Honor by her side.

"I have no idea if I'm supposed to make a toast or if that's gauche, but I don't care," Layne said. "I wanted to thank all of you, on behalf of myself and my future bride for being here. For supporting us, for loving us, and for all the work that went into tonight. So let's eat and drink, and here's to love!" she said, raising her glass.

"To love!" everyone echoed, lifting their glasses and then drinking.

"To love," I said, pulling Lark close for a kiss that tasted of champagne.

"To *our* love," she said.

I could definitely toast to that.

∽

THANKS SO FOR READING! **Reviews are SO appreciated!** They can be long or short, or even just a star rating.

∽

READ THE NEXT BOOK, Surprised By Her, where a coffee mishap leads to a kiss which leads to an unlikely relationship...

Turn the page to read a teaser of Everly and Ryan's story, which is inspired by the movie Notting Hill.

About Surprised By Her

When my boss at Bluebird Pottery, Sydney, left me in charge while she went on vacation with her girlfriend, I wasn't looking forward to it. During my first few hours, a tall, stunning stranger walked in, and I could barely breathe. Of course I ruined everything by spilling coffee all over her. What I didn't expect was for her to push me up against the sink and kiss the hell out of me when I tried to help her clean up in the bathroom.

I never thought I'd see her again, and then she showed up to my book club and introduced herself as Ryan Jewel, the heiress to a candle company fortune and is so far out of my league, we're not even on the same planet. Still, I keep running into her in Arrowbridge, and it doesn't feel like a coincidence.

At first, I'm happy to be sucked into Ryan's glittering orbit. Everything is first class all the way, and it's nice to have a little luxury in my life. Even beyond the money, I'm dazzled by her. Underneath her chilly exterior is someone who's secretly kind, and funny, and who cares fiercely for those she loves.

It doesn't take long for me to completely fall for her, but could this incredible creature ever want a small-town life with someone like me?

≈

"Good morning," I said in my cheerful, customer service voice. I'd perfected it over the past few years working retail, and it was going to be in full force this week. Sydney, my boss and manager, was currently lounging on a beach with her gorgeous girlfriend, and I was just hoping nothing went wrong. Since it was only Monday, I had a lot more hours to go.

A few people came into the shop and I made my presence known, but not too aggressively. They seemed like they were just killing time, so I let them do their thing and did my best not to hover.

The door opened again and in walked a woman who was so tall, I couldn't help but stare. She definitely wasn't from around here. I had only lived in Arrowbridge for five months, but I'd never seen anyone who looked like her. Her hair was so blonde it was almost white, and cut short on the sides and longer on top and carefully styled so she was both glam and butch at the same time.

Light blue eyes scanned the shop and then stopped when they found me.

"Good morning," I said, my voice barely audible. I cleared my throat and tried again. "Good morning, can I help you?"

She stepped closer and I took in her dark blue short-sleeve button-down, black slacks, and boat shoes.

Tall. So freaking tall. I knew I was only just above five feet, so to me, most people were tall, but she was taller.

She finally spoke. "I'm looking for a gift." Her voice was rich too. Expensive and cultured. Definitely not from here.

"We have all kinds of gift items, maybe I can help you choose something?" I asked. This was one of the best parts of my job. Second only to packing the perfect box for some reason.

She flicked her eyes over my lavender hair, which sometimes people couldn't hide their disapproval about. With her, I only caught a little surprise before she went back to walking around the shop.

"I think I can handle it on my own," she said.

I sighed inwardly. Damn. She was probably going to leave without buying anything. One of my goals this week was to sell as many things as I possibly could to show Sydney and her mom, Eileen (who was also technically my boss) that I was good at my job. They'd given me a chance and I wanted to show them it had been worth it.

"Can I get you a cup of coffee?" I asked. Some days Arrowbridge locals would come in just to grab a free cup, but actual customers loved it too, even though it was June and most people wanted iced drinks.

"Sure," she said, picking up a mug and studying the design on it before setting it back down. There were silver rings on nearly every one of her fingers. The other people who'd been wandering around left, so it was just her and me in the main part of the shop, with Eileen out back painting mugs and listening to music on her headphones.

I filled a cup with black coffee and grabbed some creamer packets and a stirring stick, as well as a cup sleeve and a napkin.

"Here you are," I said, going to hand her the cup, but I bumped her hand as she reached and the cup ended up spilling all over her front.

She jumped back, but some of the coffee had doused her shirt and pants.

"Oh my god, oh my god," I said, dropping everything. "I'm so sorry, fuck, are you okay?"

"Where's the bathroom?" she asked, and I pointed.

Her legs were so long that she made it to the bathroom quicker than I did and I stood there as she turned on the sink and started dousing herself with water.

Immediately, my thoughts went to panic. What if I'd

burned her? Was she going to sue the store? There was no way that Sydney had enough money to pay for a lawsuit and then the business was going to go under and I'd be out of a job.

She cursed a few times under her breath and then unbuttoned her shirt and pulled it off, revealing a white tank top with a beige bra underneath.

"Are you okay?" I asked again as she pulled up the shirt to reveal an absolutely ripped stomach. I'd never seen abs like that so closely before. Her skin was red in spots from where it had been splashed by the coffee.

"Fuck," I said, staring to really panic. Why had I given her coffee? Why couldn't I just have left her alone and ogled her from afar? Why did shit like this always seem to happen to me?

"Let me help you," I said, searching for any way I could salvage this situation. I grabbed some towels and wetted them with water and started pressing them against her stomach.

Strong hands took hold of my wrists and stopped me. I looked up, way up, into her face.

"I'm okay," she said. "Nothing a washing machine can't fix."

"But your skin is all red," I said.

"It's fine," she said, pushing my hands away. Oh shit, now I'd fucked up even worse by putting my hand all over her abs.

Beautiful women made me lose my mind, exhibit 400.

"I'm so sorry," I said.

"It was an accident," she said, letting go of my hands. "No harm done."

Her mouth kicked up in the briefest of smiles.

"I'm still sorry," I said. "Are you sure you're not burned?"

"The coffee wasn't that hot," she said. "No permanent damage."

"Oh," I said. "Good."

She continued to look down at me as I held the dripping towels in my hands, unable to break my gaze from hers.

I opened my mouth to say something else, but then I couldn't, because she had kissed me.

The towels fell from my grasp as the stranger shoved me against the sink and ravished my mouth.

What. Was. Happening?

Find out what happens next…

Reading List

Mistakes Were Made by Meryl Wilsner (Chapter 4)
    The Weight of the Stars by K. Ancrum (Chapter 6)
    Don't Cry for Me by Rachel Lacey (Chapter 6)
    Checking it Twice by Lucy Bexley (Chapter 9)
    Fingersmith by Sarah Waters (Chapter 12)

About the Author

Chelsea M. Cameron is a New York Times/USA Today/Internationally Best Selling author from Maine who now lives and works in Boston. She's a red velvet cake enthusiast, obsessive tea drinker, former cheerleader, and world's worst video gamer. When not writing, she enjoys watching infomercials, eating brunch in bed, tweeting, and playing fetch with her cat, Sassenach. She has a degree in journalism from the University of Maine, Orono that she promptly abandoned to write about the people in her own head. More often than not, these people turn out to be just as weird as she is.

Connect with her on Twitter, Facebook, Instagram, Bookbub, Goodreads, and her Website.

If you liked this book, please take a few moments to **leave a review**. Authors really appreciate this and it helps new readers find books they might enjoy. Thank you!

Also by Chelsea M. Cameron

The Noctalis Chronicles

Fall and Rise Series

My Favorite Mistake Series

The Surrender Saga

Rules of Love Series

UnWritten

Behind Your Back Series

OTP Series

Brooks (The Benson Brothers)

The Violet Hill Series

Unveiled Attraction

Anyone but You

Didn't Stay in Vegas

Wicked Sweet

Christmas Inn Maine

Bring Her On

The Girl Next Door

Who We Could Be

Castleton Hearts

Ingram Content Group UK Ltd.
Milton Keynes UK
UKHW020656270623
424112UK00015B/561